Harry Harrison

Wheelworld

Volume 2 in the *To the Stars* trilogy

A PANTHER BOOK

GRANADA
London Toronto Sydney New York

Published by Granada Publishing Limited in 1981

ISBN 0 586 04968 1

A Granada Paperback UK Original
Copyright © Harry Harrison 1981

Granada Publishing Limited
Frogmore, St Albans, Herts AL2 2NF
and
3 Upper James Street, London W1R 4BP
866 United Nations Plaza, New York, NY 10017, USA
117 York Street, Sydney, NSW 2000, Australia
100 Skyway Avenue, Rexdale, Ontario, M9W 3A6, Canada
PO Box 84165, Greenside, 2034 Johannesburg, South Africa
61 Beach Road, Auckland, New Zealand

Set, printed and bound in Great Britain by
Cox & Wyman Ltd, Reading
Set in Intertype Times

Granada ®
Granada Publishing ®

Jan turned to face them.

'I am going to tell you some facts, facts you cannot argue with. First, the ships are late. Four weeks late. In all the years the ships have been coming they have never been this late. Only once in all that time have they been more than four days late. The ships are late and we have used up all our time waiting. If we stay we burn. In the morning we must stop work and begin preparations for the trip.'

'The last corn in the fields . . .' someone shouted.

'Will be burned up. We leave it. We are late already . . . if we wait any longer we will die waiting. We must begin the trip south and hope they will be waiting for us when we get to Southland. It is all we can do. We must leave at once and take the corn with us . . .'

Also by Harry Harrison

Deathworld 1
Deathworld 2
Deathworld 3
The Stainless Steel Rat
The Stainless Steel Rat's Revenge
The Stainless Steel Rat Saves the World
The Stainless Steel Rat Wants You
Bill, the Galactic Hero
The Technicolor Time Machine
Make Room! Make Room!
Star Smashers of the Galaxy Rangers
The California Iceberg
Planet of the Damned
Plague from Space
The Men from P.I.G. and R.O.B.O.T.
Captive Universe
In Our Hands, The Stars
Spaceship Medic
A Transatlantic Tunnel, Hurrah!
One Step from Earth
Prime Number
Montezuma's Revenge
Queen Victoria's Revenge
Skyfall
Two Tales and Eight Tomorrows
War with the Robots
The Best of Harry Harrison
Backdrop of Stars
Planet Story (illustrated)
Great Balls of Fire (non-fiction)
Mechanismo (non-fiction)
Spacecraft in Fact and Fiction (non-fiction)
Homeworld

Chapter One

The sun had set four years ago and had not risen since.

But the time would be coming soon when it would lift over the horizon again. Within a few short months it would once more sear the planet's surface with its blue-white rays. But until that happened the endless twilight prevailed and, in that half-light, the great ears of mutated corn grew rich and full. A single crop, a sea of yellow and green that stretched to the horizon in all directions – except one. Here the field ended, bounded by a high metal fence, and beyond the fence was the desert. A wasteland of sand and gravel, a shadowless and endless plain that vanished into dimness under the twilight sky. No rain fell here and nothing grew here – in sharp contrast to the burgeoning farmland beyond. But something lived in the barren plains, a creature that found its every need in the sterile sands.

The flattened mound of creased grey flesh must have weighed at least six tonnes. There appeared to be no opening or organs in its upper surface, although close examination would have revealed that each of the nodules in the thick skin contained a silicon window that was perfectly adapted to absorb radiation from the sky. Plant cells beneath the transparent areas, part of the intricate symbiotic relationships of the lumper, transformed the energy into sugar. Slowly, sluggishly, by osmotic movement between cells, the sugar migrated to the lower portion of the creature where it was transformed into alcohol and stored in vacuoles until needed. A number of other chemical processes were also taking place on this lower surface at the same time.

The lumper was draped over a particularly rich outcropping of copper salts. Specialized cells had secreted acid to dissolve the salts, which had then been absorbed. This process had been going on for a measureless time, for the beast had no brain recognizable as such, or any organs to measure time with. It existed. It was here, eating, cropping the minerals as a cow would grass. Until, as in a grazed field, the available supply of food was gone. The time had come to move on. When the supply of nourishment fell away chemoreceptors passed on their messages and the thousands of leg muscles in the lumper's ridged lower surface began to retract. Fuelled now by the carefully stored alcohol, the muscles were actuated in a single, orgasmic spasm that sent the six tonnes of thick, carpetlike hulk hurtling over thirty metres through the air.

It cleared the fence that ringed the farm and fell with an immense thudding impact into the two metre high Gamma-corn, crushing it flat, vanishing from sight behind the screen of green leaves and arm-long, golden ears. At its largest point the lumper was only a metre thick, so it was completely hidden from view from the other creature that rumbled towards it.

Neither of them had a brain. The six-tonne organic beast was controlled completely by the reflex arcs it had been born with some centuries earlier. The metallic creature weighed twenty-seven tonnes and was controlled by a programmed computer that had been installed when it was built. Both of them had senses – but were not sentient. Each was totally unaware of the other until they met.

The meeting was very dramatic. The great form of the harvester approached, clanking and whirring industriously. It was cutting a swathe thirty metres wide through the evenly aligned rows of corn that marched away to the horizon. In a single pass it cut the corn, separated the ripe ears from the stalks, chopped the stalks to small bits, then burnt the fragments in a roaring oven. The water vapour from this instant combustion escaped from a high chimney in white trails, the ash billowed out in a black cloud from between the clanking treads to settle back to the ground. It was a very efficient machine at doing what it was supposed to do. It was not supposed to detect lumpers hidden in the corn field. It ran into the lumper and snapped off a good two hundred kilos of flesh before the alarms brought it to a halt.

Primitive as its nervous system was, the lumper was certainly aware of something as drastic as this. Chemical signals were released to activate the jumping feet and within minutes, incredibly fast for a lumper, the muscles contracted and the beast jumped again. It wasn't a very good leap though, since most of the alcohol had been exhausted. The effort was just enough to raise it a few metres into the air to land on top of the harvester. Metal bent and broke and many more alarm signals were tripped to add to the ones already activated by the beast's presence.

Wherever the gold plating of the harvester had been torn or scratched away the lumper found toothsome steel. It settled down, firmly draped over the great machine, and began to placidly eat it.

'Don't be stupid!' Lee Ciou shouted, trying to make himself heard above the babble of voices. 'Just think about stellar distances before you start talking about radio signals. Sure I could put together a big transmitter, no problem at all. I could blast out a signal that could even be received on Earth – some day. But it would take twenty-seven years to reach the nearest inhabited planet. And maybe they wouldn't even be listening . . .'

'Order, order, order,' Ivan Semenov called out, hitting the

table with the gavel in time to the words. 'Let us have some order. Let us speak in turn and be recognized. We are getting nowhere acting in this fashion.'

'We're getting nowhere in any case!' someone shouted. 'This is all a waste of time.'

There were loud whistles and boos at this and more banging of the gavel. The telephone light beside Semenov blinked rapidly and he picked up the handpiece, still banging the gavel. He listened, gave a single word of assent and hung up. He did not use the gavel again but instead raised his voice and shouted.

'Emergency!'

There was instant silence and he nodded. 'Jan Kulozik – are you here?'

Jan was seated near the rear of the dome and had not taken part in the discussion. Wrapped in his own thoughts he was scarcely aware of the shouting men, or of the silence, and had been roused only when he heard his name spoken. He stood. He was tall and wiry, and would have been thin but for the hard muscles, the result of long years of physical work. There was grease on his overalls and more smeared on his skin, yet he was obviously more than just a mechanic. The way he held himself, ready yet restrained, and the way he looked towards the chairman spoke as clearly as did the golden cogwheel symbol on his collar.

'Trouble in the fields at Taekeng-four,' Semenov said. 'Seems a lumper tangled with a harvester and knocked it out. They want you right away.'

'Wait, wait for me,' a small man called out, fighting his way through the crowd and hurrying after Jan. It was Chun Taekeng, head of the Taekeng family. He was as ill tempered as he was old, wrinkled and bald. He punched one man who did not get out of his way fast enough and kicked ankles of others to move them aside. Jan did not slow his fast walk so that Chun had to run, panting, to catch up with him.

The maintenance copter was in front of the machine shop and Jan had the turbines fired and the blade turning as Chun Taekeng climbed arthritically in.

'Ought to kill the lumpers, wipe out the species,' he gasped as he dropped into the seat by Jan. Jan did not answer. Even if there were any need, which there was not, wiping out the native species would be next to impossible. He ignored Chun, who was muttering angrily to himself, and opened the throttle wide as soon as they had altitude. He had to get there as soon as possible. Lumpers could be dangerous if they weren't handled right. Most of the farmers knew little about them – and cared even less.

The countryside drifted by below them like an undulating, yellow-specked green blanket. Harvesting was in its final stages so that the fields of corn no longer stretched away smoothly in all directions, but had been cut back in great gaps by the harvesting machines. Rising columns of vapour marked the places where the machines were working. Only the sky was unchanging, a deep bowl of unrelieved grey stretching from horizon to horizon. Four years since he had seen the sun, Jan thought, four endless and unchanging years. People here didn't seem to notice it, but at times the unchanging half-light was more than he could bear and he would reach for the little green jar of pills.

'There, down there,' Chun Taekeng called out shrilly, pointing a claw-like finger. 'Land right there.'

Jan ignored him. The shining gold hulk of the harvester was below them, half covered by the draped mass of the lumper. A big one, six, seven tonnes at least. It was usually only the smaller ones that reached the farms. Trucks and track-trucks were pulled up around it; a cloud of dust showed another one on its way. Jan circled slowly, while he put a call through on the radio for the Big Hook, not heeding Chun's orders to land at once. When he finally did set down, over a hundred metres from the harvester, the little man was beginning to froth. Jan was completely unaffected; it was the members of the Taekeng family who would suffer.

There was a small crowd gathered around the flattened harvester, pointing and talking excitedly. Some of the women had chilled bottles of beer in buckets and were setting out glasses. It was a carnival atmosphere, a welcome break from the monotony and drudgery of their lives. An admiring circle watched while a young man with a welding torch held it close to the draping curtain of brown flesh that hung down the side of the machine. The lumper rippled when the flame touched it; greasy tendrils of foul-smelling smoke rose from the burnt flesh.

'Turn off that torch and get out of here,' Jan said.

The man gaped up slackly at Jan, mouth hanging open, but did not turn off the torch or move. There was scarcely any distance between his hairline and his eyebrows and he had a retarded look. The Taekeng family was very small and inbred.

'Chun,' Jan called out to the Family Head as he tottered up, wheezing. 'Get that torch away before there is trouble.'

Chun shrieked with anger and emphasized his remarks with a sharp kick. The young man fled with the torch. Jan had a pair of heavy gloves tucked into his belt and he pulled them on. 'I'll need some help,' he said. 'Get shovels and help me lift the edge of this thing. Don't touch it underneath though. It drips acid that will eat a hole in you.'

With an effort a flap was lifted and Jan bent to look under. The flesh was white and hard, wet with acid. He found one of the many jumping legs, the size and roughly the same shape as a human leg. It was folded into a socket in the flesh and it pulled back when he dragged on it. But it

10

could not resist a continuous tension and he drew it out far enough to see the direction of bend of the stocky knee. When he released it it slowly returned to position.

'All right, let it drop.' He stepped away and scratched a mark on the ground, then turned and sighted along it. 'Get those trucks out of there,' he said. 'Move them off to left and right, at least as far away as the copter. If this thing jumps again it will land on top of them. After the burning it might just do that.'

There was some confusion as to what he meant, but no confusion when Chun repeated the orders at the top of his lungs. They moved quickly. Jan wiped his gloves on the stubble then climbed on top of the harvester. A sound of loud fluttering announced the arrival of the Big Hook. The big copter, the largest on the planet, rumbled up and hovered overhead. Jan took his radio from his belt and issued orders. A square opening appeared in the belly and a lifting bar dropped slowly down at the end of the cable. The downdraft of the rotors beat at Jan as he placed the bar carefully, then set the large hooks, one by one, into the edge of the lumper. If the creature felt the sharp steel in its flesh it gave no indication. When the hooks were set to his satisfaction, Jan circled his hand over his head and the Big Hook began to slowly lift.

Following his directions the pilot put tension on the cable, then began to carefully reel it in. The hooks sank deep and the lumper began to shiver with a rippling motion. This was the bad time. If it jumped now it could wreck the copter. But the edge came up, higher and higher, until the moist white underside was two metres in the air. Jan chopped with his hand and the Big Hook moved slowly away, towing the edge of the creature behind it level with the ground. It was like taking a blanket by the edge and turning it back. Smoothly and easily the lumper rolled until it was lying on its back on the ground, its underside a great expanse of glistening white flesh.

In a moment it changed as the thousands of legs shot suddenly into the air, an instantly grown forest of pale limbs. They stood straight up for long seconds, then slowly dropped back to rest.

'It's harmless now,' Jan said. 'It can't get off its back.'

'Now you will kill it,' Chun Taekeng said warmly.

Jan kept the distaste from his voice. 'No, we don't want to do that. I don't think you really want seven tonnes of rotting flesh in your field. We'll leave it there for now. The harvester is more important.' He radioed the Big Hook to land, then detached the lumper from the lift bar.

There was a bag of soda ash in the copter, kept there for just this kind of emergency. There was always some kind of lumper trouble. He climbed on top of the harvester again and threw handfuls of the soda ash into the pools of acid. There did not seem to be much pitting, but there could be trouble inside if the acid had dripped into the machinery. He would have to start taking the plates off at once. A number of the covers were buckled and some of the bogie wheels torn free so that it had shed one track. It would be a big job.

With the one track still powered, and four trucks towing the other side, he managed to back the harvester a good two hundred metres away from the lumper. Under the critical eye, and even more critical comments, of Chun Taekeng, he had the Big Hook drag the lumper into position and turn it over.

'Leave the ugly beast here! Kill it, bury it! Now it is right side up again and will jump again and kill us all.'

'No it won't,' Jan said. 'It can only move in one direction, you saw how the legs were aligned. When it jumps again it will be headed back for the wastelands.'

'You can't be sure, accurate . . .'

12

'Accurate enough. I can't aim it like a gun, if that's what you mean. But when it goes it is going out of here.'

Right on cue the lumper jumped. It had no reasoning power and no emotions. But it did have a complex set of chemical triggers. They must have all been activated by the rough handling it had had, the apparent reversal of gravity, burning, and having pieces removed. There was a heavy thud as all the legs kicked out at once. Some of the women screamed and even Chun Taekeng gasped and fell back.

The immense form was hurled into the air, soaring high. It cleared the field and the senser beams and fell heavily into the sand outside. A heavy cloud of dust rolled out on all sides of it.

Jan took his toolbox from the copter and set to work on the harvester, pleased to lose himself in his work. As soon as he did this, when he was left alone, his thoughts returned instantly to the ships. He was tired of thinking about them and talking about them, but he could not forget them. No one could forget them.

Chapter Two

'I don't want to talk about the ships,' Alzbeta Mahrova said. 'That's all anyone ever talks about now.'

She sat on the bench very close to Jan with the length of her thigh pressed hard against his. He could feel the warmth of her body through the thin fabric of her dress and the cloth of his overalls. He wrung his hands tightly together so that the tendons stood out like cables in his wrists. This was as close as he was ever going to get to her, here on this planet. He looked at her out of the corners of his eyes; the smooth tanned skin of her arms, the black hair to her shoulders, her eyes wide and dark too, her breasts . . .

'The ships are important,' he said, taking his eyes from her with an effort, looking without interest at the thick-walled storage building across the width of the lava road. 'They are six weeks late today, and we are four weeks late in leaving. Something must be decided tonight. Have you asked The Hradil again about our getting married?'

'Yes,' Alzbeta said, turning towards him and taking his hands in hers, even though people walking by could see them. Her eyes were dark and sorrowful. 'She refused to hear me out. I must marry someone from the Semenov Family or I must not marry. That is the law.'

'Law!' he grated the word out like an oath, pulling his hands from hers, moving away from her on the bench, tortured by her touch in a way she did not know. 'This is no law, just custom, stupid custom, peasant superstition. On this peasant planet around a blue and white star that can't even be seen from Earth. On Earth I could be married, have a family.'

'But you are not on Earth.' She spoke so softly he barely heard her.

It drained the anger from him, making him suddenly weary. Yes, he was not on Earth and would never return to Earth. He had to make his life here and find a way of bending the rules. He could not break them. His watch read twenty hours, though the endless twilight still prevailed. Though the twilight was four years long, men still measured time with their watches and clocks, with the rhythms in their bodies of a planet light years distant.

'They've been in that meeting and going at it for over two hours now, going over the same ground again and again. They should be tired.' He rose to his feet.

'What will you do?' she asked.

'What must be done. The decision cannot be put off any longer.'

She took his hand briefly in hers, letting go quickly as though she understood what the touch of her skin did to him. 'Good luck.'

'It's not me that needs the luck. My luck ran out when I was shipped from Earth on a terminal contract.'

She could not go with him because this was a meeting of the Family Heads and the technical officers only. As Maintenance Captain he had a place here. The inner door to the pressurized dome was locked and he had to knock loudly before the lock rattled and it opened. Proctor Captain Ritterspach looked out at him suspiciously from his narrow little eyes.

'You're late.'

'Shut up, Hein, and just open the door.' He had very little respect for the Proctor Captain who bullied those beneath him in rank, toadied to those above.

15

The meeting was just as demoralized as he had expected. Chun Taekeng, as Senior Elder, had the chair and his constant hammering and screaming when he was ignored did nothing to help quiet things. There was cross talk and bitter denunciations, but nothing positive was being proposed. They were repeating the same words they had been using for over a month, getting nowhere. The time had come.

Jan walked forward, holding up his hand for attention, but was ignored by Chun. He walked closer still until he stood before the small man, looming over him. Chun waved him away angrily and tried to peer round him, but Jan did not move.

'Get out of here, back to your seat, that is an order.'

'I am going to speak. Shut them up.'

The voices were dying down, suddenly aware of him. Chun hammered loudly with the gavel and this time there was silence.

'The Maintenance Captain will speak,' he called out, then threw the gavel down with disgust. Jan turned to face them.

'I am going to tell you some facts, facts you cannot argue with. First – the ships are late. Four weeks late. In all the years the ships have been coming they have never been this late. Only once in all that time have they been more than four days late. The ships are late and we have used up all our time waiting. If we stay we burn. In the morning we must stop work and begin preparations for the trip.'

'The last corn in the fields . . .' someone shouted.

'Will be burned up. We leave it. We are late already. I ask our Trainmaster Ivan Semenov if this is not true.'

'What about the corn in the silos?' a voice called out, but Jan ignored that question for the moment. One step at a time.

'Well Semenov?'

16

With reluctance the grey head nodded solemnly. 'Yes, we must leave. We must leave to keep to our schedule.'

'There it is. The ships are late and if we wait any longer we will die waiting. We must begin the trip south and hope they will be waiting for us when we get to Southland. It is all we can do. We must leave at once and we must take the corn with us.'

There was stunned silence. Someone laughed briefly then shut up. This was a new idea and they were only confused by new ideas.

'It is impossible,' The Hradil finally said, and many heads nodded in agreement. Jan looked at the angular face and thin lips of the leader of Alzbeta's family and kept his voice toneless and flat so his hatred of her would not show.

'It is possible. You are an old woman who knows nothing of these matters. I am captain in the service of science and I tell you it can be done. I have the figures. If we limit our living space during the trip we can carry almost a fifth of the corn with us. We can then empty the trains and return. If we go fast this can be done. The empty trains will be able to carry two-fifths of the corn. The rest will burn – but we will have saved almost two-thirds of the crop. When the ships come they *must* have the food. People will be starving. We will have it for them.'

They found their voices and shouted questions at him and at each other, derision and anger on all sides with the gavel banging unnoticed. He turned his back and ignored them. They would have to talk it out, walk around the new idea and spit on it a bit. Then they might begin to understand it. They were reactionary, stubborn peasants and they hated anything new. When they quietened down he would speak to them, now he kept his back turned and ignored them. Looking at the great map of the planet that hung from the dome, the only decoration in the big hall.

Halvmörk, that's what the first discovery team had called it. Twilight, the twilight world. Its name in the catalogues was officially Beta Aurigae-three, the third planet out and the only one that was habitable of the six worlds that circled the fiercely hot blue and white star. Or barely habitable. For this planet was an anomaly, something very interesting to the astronomers who had studied it and entered the facts into their records and passed on. It was the great axial tilt of the world that made it so fascinating to the scientists, almost habitable to the people who lived there. The axial tilt of forty-one degrees and the long, flattened ellipse of the orbit created a most singular situation. Earth had an axial tilt of only a few degrees, and that was enough to cause the great change in the seasons. The axis is the line about which a planet revolves; the axial tilt the degree that the axis deviates from the vertical. Forty-one degrees is a very dramatic deviation and this, combined with the long ellipse of its orbit, produced some very unusual results.

Winter and summer were each four Earth years long. For four long years there was darkness at the winter pole, the planetary pole that faced away from the sun. This ended, suddenly and drastically, when the planet turned the brief curve at one end of the elliptical orbit and summer came to the winter pole. The climatic differences were brutal and dramatic as the winter pole became the summer one, to lie exposed to the sun for four years, as it had done to the winter darkness.

While in between the poles, from forty degrees north to forty degrees south, there was endless burning summer. The temperature at the equator stayed above 200 degrees most of the time. At the winter pole the temperature remained in the thirties and there was even an occasional frost. In the extremes of temperature of this deadly planet there was only one place where men could live comfortably. The twilight

18

zone. The only habitable place on Halvmörk was this zone around the winter pole. Here the temperature varied only slightly, between seventy and eighty degrees, and men could live and crops could grow. Wonderful, mutated crops, enough to feed half a dozen crowded planets. Atomic powered desalination plants supplied the water, turning the chemicals from the rich sea into fertilizer. The terrestrial plants had no enemies, because all native life on the planet was based on copper compounds, not carbon. Each flesh was poison to the other. Nor could the copper-based plant life compete for physical space with the faster growing, more energetic carbon forms. They were squeezed out, eliminated – and the crops grew. Crops adapted to the constant, muted, unending light and unchanging temperature. They grew and grew and grew.

For four years until the summer came and the burning sun rose above the horizon and made life impossible again. But when summer arrived at one hemisphere winter fell in the other and there was another habitable twilight zone at the opposite pole. Then it would be possible to farm the other hemisphere for four years until the seasons changed again.

The planet was basically very productive once the water and the fertilizer were supplied. The local plant life presented no problems. The Earth's economy was such that getting settlers was no problem either. With the FTL drive transport costs were reasonable. When the sums had been carefully done and checked it was clear that food crops could be produced most reasonably and transported cheaply to the nearest inhabited worlds, while the entire operation was designed to show a handsome profit as well. It could be done. Even the gravity was very close to Earth norm for while Halvmörk was larger than Earth it was not nearly as dense. Everything was very possible. There were even two large land masses around the poles that contained the needed twilight zones. They could be farmed turn and turn about, for four years each. It could be done.

Except how did you get your farmers and equipment from zone to zone every four years? A distance of nearly twenty-seven thousand kilometres.

Whatever discussions and plans had been proposed were long since buried in forgotten files. But the few options open were fairly obvious. Simplest, and most expensive, would be to provide for two different work forces. While duplicating machinery and buildings would not be excessively expensive, the thought of a work force loafing in air-conditioned buildings for five years out of every nine was totally unacceptable. Unthinkable to work managers who wrung every erg of effort from their labourers with lifetime contracts. Transportation by sea must have been considered, Halvmörk was mostly ocean, except for the two polar continents and some island chains. But this would have meant land transportation to the ocean, then large expensive ships that could weather the violent tropical storms. Ships that had to be maintained and serviced to be used just once every four and a half years. Also unthinkable. Then was there a possible solution?

There was. The terraforming engineers had much experience in making planets habitable to man. They could purify poisoned atmospheres, melt icecaps and cool tropics, cultivate deserts and eliminate jungles. They could even raise land masses where desired, sink others that were not needed. These latter dramatic changes were brought about by the careful placing of gravitronic bombs. Each of these was the size of a small building and had to be assembled in a specially dug cavern deep in the ground. The manner of their operation was a secret carefully kept by the corporation that built them – but what they did was far from secret. When activated, a gravitronic bomb brought about a sudden surge of seismic activity. A planet's crust would be riven, the magma below released, which in turn brought about normal seismic activity. Of course this could only be effective where the tectonic plates overlapped but this usually allowed for a wide enough latitude of choice.

The gravitronic bombs had brought a chain of flaming volcanoes from the ocean deeps of Halvmörk, volcanoes that vomited out lava that cooled and turned to stone to form an island chain. Before the volcanic activity died down the islands became a land bridge connecting the two continents. After this it was, relatively speaking, a simple matter to lower the tallest mountains with hydrogen bombs. Simpler still was the final step of levelling the rough-shaped land with fusion guns. These same guns smoothed the surface to make a solid stone highway from continent to continent, reaching almost from pole to pole, a single road 27,000 kilometres in length.

Doing this could not have been cheap. But the corporations were all-powerful and controlled the Earth's wealth completely. A consortium could have been formed easily enough, was formed, for the returns would be high and go on for ever.

The forced settlers of Halvmörk were migrant farmers with a vengeance. For four years they laboured, raising and storing their crop against the day when the ships came. It was the long-awaited, highly exciting, most important event in the cycle of their existence. The work ended when the ships signalled their arrival. The standing corn was left in the field and the party began, for the ships also brought everything that made life possible on this basically inhospitable world. Fresh seed when needed, for the mutated strains were unstable and the farmers were not agricultural scientists who could control this. Clothing and machine parts, new radioactive slugs for the atomic engines, all the thousand and one parts and supplies that maintained a machine-based culture on a non-manufacturing planet. The ships stayed just long enough to offload the supplies and fill their holds with the grain. Then they left and the party ended. All the marriages were consummated, for this was the only time when marriage was allowed, all the celebrations finished, all the liquor drunk.

Then the trip began.

They moved like gypsies. The only permanent structures were the machine storage buildings and the thick-walled grain silos. When the partitions had been taken down and the tall doors levered open, the trucks and copters, the massive harvesters, planters and other farm machinery were wheeled inside. With their vitals cocooned and their machinery sealed in silicon grease, they would wait out the heat of the summer until the farmers returned the following fall.

Everything else went. The assembly hall and the other pressurized dome structures were deflated and packed away. When the jacks were retracted all the other narrow, long buildings settled on to the springs and wheels beneath them. The women had been canning and storing food for months, the slaughter of the sheep and cows had filled the freezers with meat. Only a few ewe lambs and cow calves would be taken; fresh herds and flocks would be raised from the sperm bank.

When everything was in place the farm tractors and trucks would haul the units into position to form the long trains, before being moth-balled and sealed into the permanent buildings and silos themselves. The engines, the main drive units, would be unjacked after four years of acting as power plants, and would rumble into place at the head of each train. With the couplings and cables connected the train would come to life. All the windows would be sealed and the air conditioning switched on. It would not be turned off again until they had reached the twilight zone of the southern hemisphere and the temperatures were bearable again. The thermometer could easily top 200° when they crossed the equator. Though the night temperatures sometimes fell as low as 130° this could not be counted upon. Halvmörk rotates in eighteen hours and the nights are too short for any real temperature drop.

'Jan Kulozik, there is a question for you. Your attention here, Kulozik, that is an order!' Chun Taekeng's voice was beginning to crack a bit after a good evening of shouting.

Jan turned from the map and faced them. There were a lot of questions but he ignored them all until the noise died down.

'Listen to me,' Jan said. 'I have worked out in detail what must be done, and I will give you the figures. But before I do you must decide. Do we take the corn or not? It is just that simple. We must leave, you cannot argue about that. And before you decide about the corn remember two things. If and when the ships come they will need that corn because people will be starving. Thousands, perhaps millions, will die if they do not get it. If we do not have that corn waiting their lives will be on our heads.

'If the ships do not come, why then we will die too. Our supplies are low, broken parts cannot be replaced, two of the engines already have lowered output and will need refuelling after this trip. We can live for a few years, but we are eventually doomed. Think about that, then decide.

'Mr chairman, I ask for a vote.'

When The Hradil rose and signalled for attention, Jan knew that it would be a long, drawn out battle. This old woman, leader of the Mahrova family, represented the strength of reaction, the force against change. She was shrewd, but she had the mind of a peasant. What was old was good, what was new was evil. All change worsened things, life must be immutable. She was listened to with respect by the other leaders, because she voiced best all their unreasoned and repetitious rationalizations. They settled down when she stood, ready for the calming balm of stupidity, the repetition as law of age-old, narrow-minded opinion.

'I have listened to what this young man has said. I value his opinion even though he is not a leader, or even a member of one of our families.' Well done, Jan thought. Take away all my credentials with your opening words, sound preparation to destroy the arguments.

'Despite this,' she continued, 'we must listen to his ideas and weigh them on their own merits. What he has said is right. It is the only way. We must take the corn. It is our ancient trust, the reason for our existence. I ask for a vote by acclamation so no one can complain later if things do not go right. I call upon you all to agree to leave at once and to take the corn. Anyone who does not agree will now stand.'

It would have taken a far stronger individual than any of those present to rise to his feet before that cold eye. And they were confused. First with a new idea, something they thought very little of at any time, much less at a time when the decision was one upon which their lives might depend. Then to have this idea supported by The Hradil, whose will was their will in almost every way. It was very disturbing. It took some thinking about, and by the time they had thought for a while it was too late to stand and face the woman, so with a good deal of irritated muttering and some dark looks the measure was carried by acclamation.

Jan did not like it, but he could not protest. Yet he was still suspicious. He was sure The Hradil hated him as intensely as he hated her. Yet she had backed his idea and forced the others into line. He would pay for this sometime, in some way he could not understand now. The hell with it. At least they had agreed.

'What do we do next?' The Hradil asked, turning in his direction but not facing him squarely. She would use him but she would not recognize him.

'We put the trains together as we always do. But before this is done the leaders here must make lists of non-essentials that can be left behind. We will go over those lists together. Then these items will be left with the machinery. Some of them will be destroyed by the heat, but we have no alternative. Two cars in every train will be used for living quarters. This will mean crowding, but it must be done. All of the other cars will be filled with corn. I have calculated this weight and the cars will carry it. The engines will go slower but, with proper precautions, they can move the trains.'

'The people will not like it,' The Hradil said, and many heads nodded.

'I know that, but you are the Family Leaders and you must make them obey. You exercise authority in every other matter, such as marriage,' he looked pointedly at The Hradil when he said this, but she was just as pointedly looking away. 'So be firm with them. It is not as though you are elected officials who can be replaced. Your rule is absolute. Exercise it. This trip will not be the easy, slow affair that it always has been. It will be fast and it will be hard. And living in the silos in Southtown will be uncomfortable until the trains return a second time. Tell the people that. Tell them now so they cannot complain later. Tell them that we will not drive the five hours a day as we have always done before, but will go on for at least eighteen hours a day. We will be going slower and we are late already. And the trains must make a second round trip. We will have very little time as it is. Now there is one other thing.'

This was the second decision they would have to make, and the most important to him personally. He hoped that Lee Ciou would do as he had agreed. The Pilot Captain did not really like people, did not like politics, and had been hard to convince that he must take a part in what was to come.

'All of this is new,' Jan said. 'There must be a co-ordinator for the changes, then the first trip, and a commander for the second trip. Someone must be in charge. Who do you suggest?'

Another decision. How they hated this. They looked around and murmured. Lee Ciou stood up, stood silently, then forced himself to speak.

'Jan Kulozik must do it. He is the only one who knows what to do.' He sat down at once.

The silence lasted long seconds while they ran the thought round and round in their minds, shocked by the newness, the break from tradition, the unexpectedness of it all.

'No!' Chun Taekeng shrieked, his face red with an anger even greater than normal, banging and banging with the gavel, unaware he was even doing it. 'Ivan Semenov will organize the trip. Ivan Semenov always organizes the trip. He is Trainmaster. That is the way it has been done, that is the way it will always be done.' Spittle flew from his lips with the violence of his words so that those in the front row leaned away, wiping surreptitiously at their faces – though nodding in agreement at the same time. This was something they could understand, neither going back nor going forward but staying with the tried and true.

'Stop that banging, Taekeng, before you break the hammer,' The Hradil said, hissing the words like a snake. The chairman gaped, he gave orders he did not take orders, this was without precedent. As he hesitated the gavel hung in mid-air and The Hradil spoke again before he could gather his thoughts.

'Better, much better. We must think of what is right, not what has been done before. This is a new thing we are doing so perhaps we will need a new organizer. I do not say we do. Perhaps. Why don't we ask Ivan Semenov what he thinks. What do you think, Ivan?'

The big man rose slowly to his feet, pulling at his beard, looking around at the technical officers and heads of families, trying to read their reactions on their faces. There was no help there. Anger, yes, and a geat deal more confusion – but no decision at all.

'Perhaps Jan should be considered, perhaps to plan if you know what I mean. Changes, they must be planned, and two trips. I really don't know . . .'

'If you don't know, shut up,' Chun Taekeng called out, banging once with the gavel for emphasis. But he had been shouting and banging all night so was ignored. Ivan went on.

'If I don't know about these changes then I will need some help. Jan Kulozik knows, it is his plan. He knows what to do. I will organize as always, but he can order the changes to be made. I must approve, yes, I insist, approval, but he could arrange the new things.'

Jan turned away so they could not see his face and know how he felt. How he tried not to, but how he hated these people. He rubbed the back of his hand across his lips to rub away some of the distaste. No one noticed, they were watching The Hradil as she spoke.

'Good. A fine plan. A Family Head must command the trip. That is the way it should be done. But the technical officer will advise. I think this is a good idea, I am for it. Anyone against it up with your hand, quick. There, all for it.'

So he was in command – but not in command. Jan had the

27

urge to stand firm, to insist on undisputed control, but this would accomplish nothing. They had bent so he must bend a bit too. Moving the corn was a necessity and that came first.

'All right,' he said, 'we'll do it that way. But there can be no arguing, we must agree upon that. Harvesting will stop at once. The cars must be stripped of every non-essential. We must cut everything by half since we will have far less than half the space we normally do. You must tell your people they have one day to make all the arrangements. If you say it like that they may be finished in two days. I want the first cars empty in two days so we can start loading the corn. Are there any questions?'

Questions? There was only silence. Do you ask a hurricane how fast it is blowing as it hurls you into the air?

Chapter Three

'I think we're leaving too early. It's a mistake.'

Hein Ritterspach fiddled with the breech of the fusion cannon, unable to look Jan in the eye. Jan slammed shut the inspection port on the reduction gear and bolted it into place. It was crowded and stuffy in the tank's driving compartment and he was aware of the other's acrid sweat.

'Not early, late if anything, Hein.' He spoke wearily, tired of repeating the same things over and over. 'The trains won't be that far behind you because we'll be moving faster. We'll catch up a lot faster than you think. That's why you will be double crewed so you can work a sixteen-hour day. I just hope it is enough. Yours is the important job, Hein. Your maintenance people in these tanks have to get over the Road ahead of us and see that it is fit to drive. You know what you are going to find. It's a job you've done before. You'll just have to work at it a bit harder this time.'

'We won't be able to move that fast. The men won't do it.'

'You'll make them do it.'

'I can't ask . . .'

'You don't ask, you *tell*.' The days of frustrating, endless work were telling on Jan. His eyes were red-rimmed and he was perpetually tired. Tired of cajoling, prodding, pushing, forcing these people to do something different just once in their lives. His temper was rubbed raw as well and the sight of this whining, pudgy idiot was too much. He spun about and poked the man deep in the blubbery gut with his finger.

'You're a complainer, Hein, do you know that? No one needs a Proctor Captain here, they are too busy and too tired to get into trouble. So you loaf. Only when we move the trains do you do any real work. Now you have got to get out ahead of us and clear the Road and that is all you have to do. So stop finding excuses and get on with the job.'

'You can't talk to me like that!'

'I just did. Your tanks and men are ready to roll. I've checked the equipment myself and it's all on line. Yet this is the third time I have checked this command tank and there is *nothing* wrong with it. So move out.'

'You, you . . .'

The big man was wordless with rage, raising a large fist over his head. Jan stepped close to him, closing a hard, scarred mechanic's fist, waiting, smiling.

'Yes, do hit me, why don't you?'

He had to speak through his teeth, his jaw was so tightly clamped, and his arm shook with restrained tension. Hein could not face him. His fist dropped and he turned away and climbed clumsily down through the hatch, his boots clattering on the rungs outside.

'That's the end of you, Kulozik!' he shouted up, his red face framed by the hatch. 'I'm going to Semenov, to Chun Taekeng. You're getting thrown out, you've gone too far . . .'

Jan took one weary step forward and raised his fist and the face vanished instantly. Yes, he had gone too far, had shown the bully to be a coward. Hein would never forgive him. Particularly since there had been a witness. Lajos Nagy sat in the co-driver's seat in silence, silent but well aware of what had happened.

'Start the motors,' Jan said. 'You think I was too hard on him, Lajos?'

'He's all right when you work with him a while.'

'I'll bet he's worse the longer he's around.'

30

A deep vibration shook the floor as the gear trains were engaged and Jan cocked his head, listening. The tank was in good shape. 'Pass the word to the others, start engines,' he said. He dogged the hatch shut as the air conditioner came on, then slid into the driver's seat, his feet on the brakes, his hands resting lightly on the wheel that synchronized track speed and clutches. Twenty tons of machinery vibrated gently with anticipation, waiting for his command.

'Tell them to stay in line behind me, at hundred-metre intervals. We're moving out.'

Lajos hesitated for just an instant before he switched on his microphone and relayed the order. He was a good man, one of Jan's mechanics when they weren't on the Road.

Jan eased the wheel forward and tilted it at the same time. The whine of the gearboxes grew in pitch and the tank lurched ahead as the clutches engaged, the heavy tracks slapping down on the solid rock of the Road. When he switched on the rear camera he saw the rest of the tanks rumble to life on the screen and move out behind him. They were on the way. The broad central street of the city slipped past, the looming walls of the warehouses, then the first of the farms beyond. He kept the controls on manual until the last of the buildings was behind him and the Road had narrowed. The tank picked up speed as he switched to automatic and sat back. A wire, embedded beneath the congealed lava surface of the Road, acted as a guide. The column of tanks roared on past the farms towards the desert beyond.

They were into the sandy wastes, the unreeling ribbon of Road the only sign of mankind's existence, before the expected message came through.

'I'm having radio trouble, I'll call you back,' Jan said, switching off the microphone. The other tanks were on FM command frequency so should not have intercepted the message. Now that he had started this thing he was going to finish it in his own way.

They were over 300 kilometres from the settlement before they hit the first problem. Sand had drifted across the Road forming a barrier two metres deep at its highest. Jan halted the column while his tank crawled up the slope. It wasn't too bad.

'Which are the two with the biggest dozer blades?'

'Seventeen and nine,' Lajos said.

'Get them up here to clean this stuff away. Get a second driver from the house car, have him stay with you until Hein Ritterspach gets here. He won't be bearable for a couple of days so try to ignore him. I'll radio for him to come in a copter, if it's not on the way already, and I'll go back with it.'

'I hope there won't be trouble.'

Jan smiled, tired but happy at having done something. 'Of course there will be trouble. That's all there ever is. But this column is moving fine, Ritterspach won't dare turn back now. All he can do is push on.'

Jan sent the message then kicked open the hatch and climbed down on to the sand. Was it warmer here – or just his imagination? And wasn't it lighter on the southern horizon? It might very well be, dawn wasn't that far away. He stood aside while the tanks ground up the slope and churned past him, the last in the column towing the house car stopping just long enough for the relief driver to climb down. The dozers were just attacking the sand when the flutter of the helicopter could be heard above the sound of their tracks. It had been on the way well before his message had been received. It circled once then settled slowly on to the Road: Jan went to meet it.

Three men climbed down and Jan knew that the trouble was not over, was perhaps just beginning. He spoke first, hoping to throw them off balance.

32

'Ivan, what the devil are you doing here? Who is taking care of things with both of us out on the Road?'

Ivan Semenov twisted his fingers in his beard and looked miserable, groping for words. Hein Ritterspach, an assistant Proctor close by his side, spoke first.

'I'm taking you back, Kulozik, under official arrest. You are going to be charged with . . .'

'Semenov, exert your authority,' Jan called out loudly, turning his back on the two Proctors, well aware of the side-arms that both men wore, their hands close to the butts. There was a tightness between his shoulder blades that he tried to ignore. 'You are Trainmaster. This is an emergency. The tanks are clearing the Road. Hein must be with them, he is in command. We can talk about his little problems when we get to Southtown.'

'The tanks can wait, this must be done first! You attacked me!'

Hein was shaking with rage, his gun half drawn. Jan turned sideways enough to watch both Proctors. Semenov finally spoke.

'A serious matter this. Perhaps we had all better return to town and discuss it quietly.'

'There is no time for discussion – or quiet.' Jan shouted the words, pretending anger to feed the other's anger as well. 'This fat fool is under my command. I never touched him. He's lying. This is mutiny. If he does not *instantly* rejoin the tanks I shall charge him and disarm him and imprison him.'

The slash of the words was of course too great a burden for Hein to bear. He pawed at his holster, clutched his gun and drew it. As soon as the muzzle was clear, before it could be raised, Jan acted.

He turned and grabbed Hein's wrist with his own right hand, his left hand slapping hard above the other's elbow. Still turning, using speed and weight, he levered the man's arm up beside his back so hard that Hein howled with pain.

Uncontrollably the big man's fingers went limp, the gun began to drop – and Jan kept pushing. It was cruel, but he must do it. There was a cracking sound that shuddered Hein's body as the arm broke and, only then, did Jan let go. The gun clattered on the stone surface of the Road and Hein slid down slowly after it. Jan turned to the other armed man.

'I am in command here, Proctor. I order you to aid this wounded man and take him into the copter. Trainmaster Semenov concurs with this order.'

The young Proctor looked from one to the other of them in an agony of indecision. Semenov, confused, did not speak, and his silence gave the man no guide. Hein groaned loudly with pain and writhed on the unyielding rock. With this reminder the Proctor decided; he let his half-drawn gun drop back into the holster and knelt beside his wounded commander.

'You should not have done that, Jan.' Semenov shook his head unhappily. 'It makes things difficult.'

Jan took him by the arm and drew him aside. 'Things were already difficult. You must take my word that I never attacked Hein. I have a witness to back me up if you have any doubts. Yet he built this trouble up so that one of us had to go. He is expendable. His second in command, Lajos, can take over. Hein will ride in the train and his arm will knit and he'll cause more trouble at Southtown. *But not now.* We must move as planned.'

There was nothing for Semenov to say. The decision had been taken from him and he did not regret it. He took the medical bag from the copter and attempted to fit an airbag splint on to the broken arm. They could only do this after an injection had put the wailing Hein under. The return trip was made in silence.

Chapter Four

Jan lay back on his bunk, his muscles too tired to relax, going over his lists just one more time. They were only hours away from departure. The last of the corn was being loaded now. As the silos were emptied the partitions were removed so that the heavy equipment could be rolled in. Coated with silicon grease and cocooned with spun plastic, they would sit out the 200 degrees' heat of the four-year long summer. All of them, trucks, copters, reapers, were duplicated and in storage at Southtown so need not be carried with them on the trek. They had their stocks of frozen food, the chicks, lambs and calves to start anew the herds and flocks, home furnishings – now painfully reduced – and the corn filling almost all the cars. The water tanks were full; he wrote and underlined: *Water*. First thing in the morning he must hook into the computer relay and put the Northpoint desalination plant on standby. It had already stopped all secondary functions, chemical and mineral extraction, fertilizer production, and was operating at minimum to keep the 1300-kilometre-long canal and tunnel complex filled with water. He could stop that now; the farming was over for this season. There was a knock on the door, so soft at first that he wasn't sure he had heard it. It was repeated.

'Just a moment.'

He pushed the sheets of paper together into a rough heap and dropped them on to the table. His legs were stiff as he shuffled across the plastic floor in his bare feet and opened the door. Lee Ciou, the radio technician stood outside.

'Am I bothering you, Jan?' He seemed worried.

'Not really. Just rattling papers when I should be sleeping.'

'Perhaps another time . . .'

'Come in, now you're here. Have a cup of tea and then maybe we'll both get some sleep.'

Lee bent and picked up a box that had been out of sight beside the door and brought it in with him. Jan busied himself with boiling water from the kitchen tap, hotting the pot then adding tea leaves to brew. He waited for Lee to talk first. Lee was a quiet man with a mind like one of his own printed circuits. Thought was processed back and forth emerging only after a measured period of time, complete and final.

'You are from Earth,' he finally said.

'I think that is a pretty well known fact. Milk?'

'Thank you. On Earth, I understand, there are many levels of society, not just a single population as we have here?'

'You might say that. It's a varied society, you've seen a lot of it on the programmes from Earth. People have different jobs, live in different countries. Lots of variety.'

Lee's forehead had a fine beading of sweat; he was disturbed, uncomfortable. Jan shook his head wearily and wondered just where this was all leading.

'Are there criminals too?' Lee asked, and Jan was suddenly very much awake.

Careful, Jan thought, be very careful. Don't say too much; don't commit yourself.

'There probably must be some. There are police after all. Why do you ask?'

'Have you ever known criminals, or people who have broken the law?'

Jan could not stay quiet. He was too tired, his nerves rubbed too raw.

'Are you a narkman? Is that your job here?' His voice was flat and cold. Lee raised his eyebrows but his expression did not change.

'Me? No, of course not. Why should I send reports to off-world police about things that happen on Halvmörk?'

You've given yourself away there, my boy, Jan thought. When he spoke again he was as cool as the other.

'If you're not a narkman – how do you know what the term means? It's an earthy slang term that is not in good repute. It mocks authority. I've never seen it on a 3V tape or read it in a book approved for use on this world.'

Lee was uncomfortable now, wringing his hands together slowly, his tea forgotten. He spoke reluctantly, yet when he did it all came out in a rush.

'You could tell, of course, you know about these things. You know what Earth, other places are like. I have long wanted to talk to you about it but thought it would be an affront. You have never talked yourself, you must have good reasons. That is why I am here tonight. Hear me out, please, do not tell me to leave yet. I mean no insult. But – your presence here – the fact you have stayed all these years means, perhaps, you cannot leave. Yet I know you are an honest man, one of good will. I do not think you are a narkman. It is a thing you would not do. If you are not that then, you are no criminal, no, but, you ... well, perhaps ...'

His voice trailed away; these things were no easier to talk about here than they were back on Earth.

'You mean that even if I am not a criminal I must be on this planet for some reason?' Lee nodded rapidly. 'Is there any reason why I should talk to you about it? It is really none of your business.'

'I know,' Lee said desperately. 'I should not ask you, I am sorry. But it is very important to me ...'

'Important to me too. I could get into trouble talking to

you – get you into difficulties too. Don't let anything I tell you go any further . . .'

'I won't – I promise!'

'Then, yes, I was in trouble with the authorities. I was sent here as punishment of a kind. And I can live here as you see me as long as I don't make any waves. Such as telling you things like this.'

'I don't mean to ask – but I must. I had to know. There is something I must tell you. I am taking a chance but I feel that the odds are right. I must tell you or give up everything – and that is something that I could not bear.' Lee straightened up and lifted his face as though waiting for a blow. 'I have broken the law.'

'Well good for you. You are probably the only one on this primitive planet with the nerve to do it.'

Lee gaped. 'This does not bother you?'

'Not in the slightest. If anything I admire you for it. What have you done that bothers you so?'

Lee lifted the flap of his jacket pocket and took out something small and black and passed it to Jan. It was thin and rectangular and had a row of tiny studs along one edge. 'Press the second one,' he said. Jan did and quiet music poured out.

'I made it myself, my own design, but with parts from supply. Not enough for anyone to ever notice. Instead of tape I use a digital memory store on a molecular level, that is why it can be so small. It will record music, books, anything, with perhaps a thousand hours easily accessible.'

'This is very good, but not what I would call a criminal act. Since the first man worked on the first machine I imagine mechanics have been using bits and pieces for their own ends. The amount of materials you have used will neither be heeded nor missed, and I do admire your design. I don't think you can call this breaking the law.'

38

'This is just the beginning.' Lee took the box from the floor and put it on the table. It was made of a pale alloy, machine-turned and held together by rows of tiny rivets, the construction a labour of love in itself. He worked the combination and opened the lid, tilting it towards Jan. It was filled with row after row of tape cassettes.

'These are from the men who land with the supply ships,' he said. 'I have been trading my recorders for these. They are very popular and I get more of them each time. There is one man who gets me all I can use. I think that is illegal.'

Jan sat back heavily and nodded. 'That is indeed against the law, against how many laws you don't know. You shouldn't mention this to anyone else, and if I am ever asked I have never heard of you. The simplest thing that would happen to you if you were discovered would be instant death.'

'That bad?' Lee was paler now, sitting bolt upright.

'That bad. Why are you telling me this?'

'I had an idea. It doesn't matter now.' He stood and picked up the box. 'I had better be going.'

'Wait.' As soon as he thought about it Jan knew why the radio technician had come. 'You are afraid of losing the tapes, aren't you? If you leave them behind the heat will destroy them. And the Elders are checking all personal luggage, as they have never done before, and they'll want to know what you have in the box. So how do you expect me to help?'

Lee did not answer because this was obvious as well.

'You were going to ask me to conceal them in my equipment for you? Risk death for blackdirt tapes?'

'I didn't know.'

'I guess not. Here, sit down, you're getting me nervous standing there. Pour the tea into the sink and I'll give you something better to drink. Just as illegal as the tapes though with not the same penalties attached.'

Jan unlocked a cabinet and took out a plastic bottle filled with a lethal looking transparent liquid. He filled two tumblers and passed one to Lee.

'Drink up – you'll like it.' He raised his own glass and drained half of it. Lee sniffed suspiciously at the glass, then shrugged and drank a good mouthful. His eyes widened and he managed to swallow it without choking.

'That's . . . that's something I never tasted before. Are you sure that it is drinkable?'

'Very much so. You know those apples I raise behind the shop? The little ones about the size of your thumb? Very sweet they are and the juice ferments easily with the right yeast strain. I get an apple wine that must be about twelve per cent alcohol. Then I put it into the deep freeze and throw away the ice.'

'Very ingenious.'

'I admit it's not an original idea of mine.'

'But it's such a simple way of concentrating the alcohol. In fact, after drinking a bit it tastes better and better.'

'That's not original either. Here, let me top you up. Then you can show me some of those tapes.'

Lee frowned. 'But the death penalty?'

'Let us say my first fright has vanished. It was just reflex. With the ships late – and they may never arrive at all – why should I worry about the retribution of Earth, light years away?' He flipped through the tapes, squinting at some of the titles. 'All pretty innocuous stuff, red hot by this planet's standards, but nothing political at all.'

'What do you mean, political?'

Jan poured their glasses full again and stared into his. 'You're a rube,' he said. 'A hick. And you don't even know what those words mean. Have you ever heard me talk about Earth?'

'No. But I never thought about it And we know about Earth from the taped shows and . . .'

'You know nothing at all here on Halvmörk. This is a dead-end planet, a concentration camp world at the end of nowhere, been nowhere, going nowhere. Settled by forced migration, probably, or with political prisoners. Doesn't matter, it's in the records someplace. Just an agricultural machine filled with dumb farmers designed to churn out food for the other planets for maximum profit at minimum input. Earth. Now that is something else again. With the elite on top, the proles on bottom and everyone in between fitted into place like plugs into a board. No one really likes it, except those at the top, but they have all of the power so things just go on and on for ever. It is a trap. A morass. With no way out. I am out of it because I had no choice. This planet – or death. And that is all I am going to tell you. So leave the tapes. I'll take care of them for you. And why the hell should we worry ourselves about something as trivial as tapes?' He banged his glass down with sudden anger.

'Something is *happening* out there – and I don't know what it is. The ships always arrive on time. Yet they haven't. They may never come. But if they do, we have the corn and they will need it . . .'

Fatigue and alcohol dragged him down. He finished the last swallow in his glass and waved Lee towards the door. Lee turned back before opening it.

'You didn't say anything to me tonight,' Lee said.

'And I never saw any damn tapes. Good night.'

Jan knew that a full three hours had gone by, but it seemed that the light and the buzzer clawed him awake just seconds

41

after his head hit the pillow. He wiped at his encrusted eyelids and was all too aware of the vile taste in his mouth. And it was going to be a very long day. As his tea was brewing he shook two stims out of the bottle, looked at them, then added a third. A very long day.

There was a heavy knocking on the door before he had finished his tea, and it was thrown open before he could reach it. One of the Chuns, he had forgotten his name, thrust his head in.

'All the corn loaded. Except this car. Like you said.' His face was streaked with grime and sweat and he looked as tired as Jan felt.

'All right. Give me ten minutes. You can start cutting the hatches now.'

Lee's illegal tapes were in with the machine tools, sealed and locked. All the clothes and personal items he would need were in a bag. As he washed the tea things and stowed them in their cabinet niches there was a burst of ruddy light from the ceiling. The point turned into a line and began to trace a circle in the metal. As he pushed his bed, table and chairs out through the front door the circle was complete and the disc of metal clanged down, biting deep into the plastic flooring. Jan threw his bag over his shoulder and left, locking the door behind him.

His machine shop car was the last to go. It seemed that everyone was working at once. A thick tube snaked over from the nearest silo and up the side of the car. The man above called out and waved and the hose writhed as the flow began. It bucked in the man's hand and a golden rain clattered down on Jan before the man leaned his weight against it and sent the corn flowing down into the car through the newly cut hole. Jan picked a kernel from his shoulder. It was as long as his middle finger, wrinkled from vacuum dehydration. A miracle food, product of the laboratories, rich in protein, vitamins, nutrition. It could be made into a child's first meal, a grown man's food, an old man's gruel and it would be all the nutrition he would need in that lifetime. A perfect food. For economic slaves. He put it into his mouth and chewed ruminently on its hard form. The only thing wrong was that it just did not taste like very much of anything.

Metal creaked as the corner jacks lifted the car above its concrete bed. Men were already in the black pit below, shouting curses as they stumbled in the darkness, lowering the wheels and locking them into position. It was all happening at once. They scrambled up the ramp at the end just as the tugtank was backing into position. While it was being hooked up, the corn loaders on the roof topped off and the pumping stopped. So well co-ordinated were the activities that the men who sealed plastic sheets over the newly cut ports actually found themselves riding on the roof, shouting protests, as the car was pulled forward slowly, rising as it rode up the ramp. Once it was on the level the brakes were locked while the mechanics crawled beneath its massive bulk to check the tyres, unseen for four years.

While Jan slept the trains had been formed up. This was only the third time he had seen the great migration and he was as impressed as he had been on the first occasion. The native Halvmörkers took it for granted, though there was excitement at the change in the daily pace of their lives. The move was just as exciting for Jan, more so perhaps since he had been accustomed to the variety and novelty of travel on Earth. Here any escape from the boredom and repetition of everyday life was a relief. Particularly with this unexpected change, this altering of the physical world he had grown to accept since they had arrived. A few days ago this had been a thriving city, surrounded by farms that stretched to the horizon and beyond. Now it had all changed. All of the bustling transport and machines had been locked away in the massive silos, their doors sealed. The domed pressure buildings had been deflated and sealed away as well. The other buildings, the mobile ones, had changed in character completely. No longer earthbound structures, they had risen on rows of sturdy wheels and been formed into regular lines, along with the farm buildings which had been trundled in to join them. Where the city had been there now stood just foundations, as though it had been wiped away in some incredible blast.

On the wide, Central Way there now stood a double row of trains. The buildings, which had seemed so varied as homes and shops, with their canopies and stairs and flowers, now proved all to be of the same size and shape. Cars in a large train, connected together and uniform. Twelve cars to a train, and each train headed by an engine. An incredible engine.

Big. At times Jan still found it hard to believe that a power plant this size could actually move. And power plants they were for all of the time they were off the Road. Jacked up and stationary, their atomic generators producing all the electricity the city and farms could possibly need, waiting patiently for their transformation back into the engines they really were.

Big. Ten times bigger than the biggest truck Jan had ever seen before coming to this planet. He slapped the tyre of one as he passed, solid and hard, the top of the tread so high above his head that he could not reach it. Lug nuts the size of dinner plates. Two steerable wheels in front, four driving wheels in back. Behind the front wheels were the rungs up to the driving compartment. Fifteen of them climbing up the burnished golden metal of the solidly riveted side of the beast. In front the battery of headlights, bright enough to blind a man in an instant if he were fool enough to stand and look at them. There was a glitter of glass from the drivers' compartment, high above. Out of sight on top were the banked rows of tubes and fins that cooled the atomic engines. Engines large enough to light a small city. He couldn't resist slamming his hand against the hard metal as he passed. It was something to drive one of these.

Ivan Semenov was waiting by the leading train.

'Will you drive engine one?' he asked.

'That's your job, Ivan, the most responsible one. The Trainmaster sits in that seat.'

Ivan's grin was a little twisted. 'Whatever titles are given, Jan, I think we know who is Trainmaster on this trip. People are talking. Now that the work has been done they think you were right. They know who is in charge here. And Hein has few friends. He lies in bed and rubs the cast on his arm and will talk to no one. People pass his car and laugh.'

'I'm sorry I did that. But I still think it was the only way.'

'Perhaps you are right. In any case they all know who is in charge. Take engine one.'

He turned on his heel and walked away before Jan could answer.

Engine one. It was a responsibility that he could handle. But there was an excitement there as well. Not only to drive one of these great brutes – but to drive the very first. Jan could not help smiling at himself as he walked faster and faster down the lengths of the trains, to the first train. To the first engine.

The thick door to the engine compartment was open and he saw the engineer bent over the lubrication controls. 'Stow this, will you,' he said as he slung his bag in through the doorway. Without waiting for an answer he grabbed the rungs and pulled himself up on to the first. To his left was the empty Road surrounded by the barren farms, more and more of the Road appearing as he climbed higher. Behind him the dual row of trains, solid and waiting. He pulled himself through the hatch into the driving compartment.

The co-driver was in his seat leafing through his checklists. In the adjoining compartment the communications officer was at his banked radios.

In front the expanse of the armoured glass window, a bank of TV screens above it. Below this, row after row of instruments and gauges that fed back information on the engine and the train it towed, and the trains behind that.

In front of the controls the single, empty chair, solid steel with padded seat, back and headrest. Before it the wheel and the controls. Jan slid slowly into it, feeling its strength against his back, letting his feet rest lightly on the pedals, reaching out and taking the cool form of the wheel in his hand.

'Start the checklist,' he said. 'Ready to roll.'

Chapter Five

Hour after frustrating hour passed. Although the trains appeared to be joined up and ready to begin the trek, there were still hundreds of minor problems that had to be solved before the starting signal could be given. Jan grew hoarse and frustrated shouting into the radiophone, until he finally slammed the headset back into the rack and went to see for himself. Fitted into a niche at the rear of the engine was a knobbly-tyred motorcycle. He unclamped it and disconnected the power lead to the battery – then found both tyres flat. Whoever should have checked it, hadn't. There was more delay while the engineer, Eino, filled a compressed air cylinder. When he finally mounted the cycle Jan had the pleasure of twisting the rheostat on full and hearing the tyres shriek as they spun against the road surface and hurled him forwards.

As Maintenance Captain, Jan's responsibility had been to keep the machinery repaired and in preparation for this day. Physically, it was impossible for him to do alone, and he had had to rely upon others to carry out his orders. Too often they had not. The multiple connectors on the thick cables that connected the cars should all have been sealed with moisture-proof lids. Many of them had not. Corrosion had coated them with non-conducting scale in so many places that over half of the circuits were dead. After crawling under car after car himself he issued an order to all the trains that *all* connectors were to be opened and cleaned with the hand sandblasts. This postponed their departure by another hour.

There were steering problems. The lead wheels of every car could swivel, turned by geared down electric motors. These wheels were controlled by the engine computer in each train so that every car followed and turned exactly as the engine had done, moving as precisely as if they were on tracks. Fine in theory but difficult in practice with worn motor brushes and jammed gear trains. Time trickled away.

There were personal difficulties as well, with everyone jammed into a fraction of the normal living space. Jan heard the complaints with one ear and nodded and referred all problems to the Family Heads. Let them earn their keep for a change. One by one he tracked down the troubles and saw them tackled and solved. The very last thing was a missing child which he found himself when he saw a movement in the corn field near by. He plunged in with the bike and restored the happy toddler, riding before him, to its weeping mother.

Tired, yet with a feeling of satisfaction, he rode slowly back between the double row of trains. The doors were sealed now and the only people in sight were the few curious faces peering from the windows. Eino, his engineer, was waiting to stow the cycle while he climbed back up to the driving compartment.

'Pre-drive checklist done,' his co-driver said. Otakar was as efficient as the machine he commanded. 'Full on line power available, all systems go.'

'All right. Get readiness reports on the other trains.'

While Jan threw switches and went through his driver's checklist he heard the reports from the other trains in his earphones. There was a hold with thirteen, a red on the safety standby circuits, which turned out to be an instrument readout failure which was corrected easily enough. They cleared one by one.

'All trains ready, all drivers ready,' Otakar said.

'Good. Communications, give me a circuit to all drivers.'

'Through,' Hyzo, the communications officer, said.

'All drivers.' As he spoke the words Jan had a sensation stronger than anything he had ever felt before. Mountain climbing, sailing – making love – each of them had produced moments of pure pleasure, of emotions both wonderful and indescribable. Only drugs had made him feel this way before, drugs that he had stopped taking because they were an easy shot, something that anyone could buy and share. But they could not share this with him because he was alone. In control of everything. Right at the top. More in control than he had ever been at any time back on Earth. He had had responsibility, more than enough of it, but never this much. Out in front, the very first, with the population of an entire world waiting for his decision to be made.

He was in charge.

The solid frame of the engine beneath him hummed lightly with the still restrained power of the engine. Heavy couplings and a web of cables connected it to the car behind and to the others behind that. Then there were the other engines and their trains, filled with the goods of this planet and all of its inhabitants. Every person, apart from the maintenance crews were there, waiting for his order. He felt the sudden dampness of his palms and wrapped his hands tightly about the hard steering wheel in front of him. The moment passed and he was in control again.

'All drivers.' Jan's voice was as calm and businesslike as it always was. His internal feelings were still his own. 'We're moving out. Set your proximity radar at one kilometre. No variations permitted above 1100 metres or below 900. Set automatic braking controls for 950. If – for *any* reason – we have an engine less than 900, and I mean 899 and down, from the train ahead we will have a new driver. No exceptions. Minimum acceleration on starting up and watch the stress gauges on your couplings. We're carrying at least twice our normal loaded weight and we can pull those couplings out like rotten teeth without even trying. Right now we are going to use a new manoeuvre and I want it used every time we start. Co-drivers enter it into your checklists. Ready to copy.

'One. All car brakes off.

'Two. Set brakes on last car.

'Three. Select reverse gear.

'Four. Reverse minimum speed for five seconds.'

This was a trick he had learned in his cadet days when he was doing maintenance on the freight monorails under the city. Backing up took up all the play in the joints and couplings. Then, when the train started forward, the entire weight of the train would not have to be set into motion at the same time, but bit by bit as the play was taken up. In this way inertia actually aided the starting up, rather than retarding it, as the weight of the cars already in motion was used to accelerate those still at rest.

With the heel of his hand Jan pushed the gear selector into reverse, then set the speed regulator at the first notch. All the brakes in the train were off except for the red light glowing on car twelve. When he stepped on the throttle with his left foot he felt the acceleration of the gear trains and a heavy shuddering through the metal of the floor. The coupling strain gauges dropped to zero, then reversed. *Skid* blinked on and off on twelve's panel and he killed the power as the digital readout of the clock read five.

'Prepare to move out,' he said and pulled the gear selector into *low range*. 'Second file of trains hold position until the last of file one has passed. Then fall in in position behind. All controls on manual until you are notified otherwise. First stop in nineteen hours. Final stop in Southtown. See you all there.'

He took the wheel firmly in both hands and let his foot rest on the accelerator.

'Move out!'

Jan stepped down slowly and the engine revved up. At speed the hydraulic clutch engaged and the torque was transmitted to the drive wheels. They turned and the engine moved ahead, car after car being set into motion behind it, until the whole giant train was rolling slowly forwards. To his left the lead engine of the second file slid back and out of sight and ahead was only the empty expanse of the Road. The rear scanner mounted on top of the engine showed the train following smoothly behind. The screen next to it, hooked to the scanner in the last car, showed engine two dropping behind. Strain gauges were all well into the green. Engine speed and road speed moved up to the top of the low range and he shifted to middle.

'All green,' Otakar said. He had been monitoring all the other readouts from the co-driver's seat. Jan nodded and turned the steering wheel to the left, then centred it again to hold the turn. Unlike the smaller ground cars the powered steering was set by displacement of the wheel and held in position by centring. He then turned the steering wheel right to straighten the wheels again and centred it when they were at zero degrees forward. Then he came right to align the engine in the centre of the Road, centred over the control cable buried under the rock surface. The cars of the train behind each turned at precisely the same spot in the same way, like a monotrain going through switches.

Jan kept the speed at the top of the middle range until all the trains had begun to move, strung out in position one kilometre apart. The city site and even the farms had vanished behind before the last train was moving. Only then did he accelerate into the highest, road speed range. The tyres hummed below, the Road rushed towards him, the featureless sandy desert moved by on each side. He held the wheel, driving still on manual, guiding the engine, the train, all of the trains down the Road, south, towards the opposite continent and Southtown still 27,000 kilometres away.

One of the few outstanding features in this stretch of desert appeared as a speck on the horizon and slowly grew as they raced towards it. A black spire of rock pointing a dark finger at the sky. It reared up from a ridge so massive that the Road took a slow swing out and round it. As it passed Jan signalled for the all-driver circuit.

'Needle Rock coming up on your left. Mark it. As you pass you can go on autopilot.'

He set the controls himself as he talked, feeding in maximum and minimum speeds with his left hand, max and min acceleration and braking as well. The gridded scope screen on the autopilot showed that he was centred over the central cable. He flipped the switch to on and leaned back. Realizing that he was stiff from the strain, kneading his fingers together.

'A good start,' Otakar said, still looking at the readouts. 'It will project to a good trip.'

'I only hope you're right. Take the con while I stretch.'

Otakar nodded and slipped into the driver's seat when Jan stood up. His muscles creaked when he flexed his arms and he walked back to the rear compartment to look over the communication officer's shoulder.

'Hyzo,' he said, 'I want a . . .'

'I have a red here,' Otakar called out sharply.

Jan spun about and ran to lean over the co-driver's shoulder. A red light had appeared, flashing among the rows of green, and a brief instant later there was a second, then a third.

'Brake drum heat on cars seven and eight. What the devil can that mean? All brakes are off.' Jan muttered savagely to himself, things had been going too well, and leaned forward to press the readout button. Numbers appeared on the screen. Up over twenty degrees on both those cars – and still rising.

He thought quickly. Should he stop and investigate? No, that would mean halting the entire line of trains, then getting them moving again. There were at least 300 kilometres more of desert road before they hit the foothills and he wouldn't be needing brakes at all until that time.

'Kill the brake circuits in both those cars and see what happens,' he said.

Otakar hit the switches as Jan was still issuing the order. Now the two cars no longer had operating brakes, but the safety circuits should have gone dead in the off position. They did. The temperature in the brake drums dropped slowly until, one after the other, the red lights went out.

'Keep the con,' Jan said, 'while I see if I can figure out just what the hell is going on.' He went to the rear and threw up the cover of the hatch down to the engine compartment. 'Eino,' he called through the opening. 'Pass me up the diagrams and manuals on the car brake circuits. We have a problem.'

Jan had done maintenance on the brake systems, as he had on all the machinery, but had never needed to break down and repair one of the systems. Like all of the Halvmörk machines these had been designed to last for ever. Or as close to that as possible. With replacement supplies light years away rugged design was a necessity. All components were simply designed and heavily built. Lubrication was automatic. They were designed not to fail under normal use and, in practice, rarely did.

'These what you want?' Eino asked, popping out of the hatch like an animal out of its den. He had diagrams and service manuals in his hand.

'Spread them out on the desk and we'll take a look,' Jan said.

The diagrams were detailed and exact. There were two separate braking systems on the cars, each with its own fail-safe mode. Normal braking was electronically controlled by the computer. When the engine driver hit the brake the brakes in all the cars were applied at the same time, to the same degree. The brakes themselves were hydraulic, the pressure coming from reservoirs that were supplied by pumps turned by the axles of the car. Strong springs held them in the normally *off* position. The electronic controls opened the pressure valves to apply the brakes when needed. This was alpha, the active braking system. Beta, the passive one, was for emergencies only. These completely separate brakes were held in the *on* position by their springs until the electric circuits were actuated. When this was done powerful magnets pulled them free. Any break in the electrical circuits, such as an accidental uncoupling of the cars, would apply these brakes for an emergency stop.

'Jan, two other trains calling in for advice,' Hyzo said. 'Sounds like the same trouble, temperature rise in the brakes.'

'Tell them to do what we did. Cut the power to the alpha systems. I'll get back to them after I track down the malfunction.' He traced the diagram with his finger. 'It *must* be the alpha brake system. The emergencies are either full on or full off – and we would certainly know if they were on.'

'Electronics or hydraulics?' the engineer asked.

'I have a feeling that it can't be the electronics. The computer monitors all those circuits. If there were an uncalled for on-brake signal it would negate it, and if it couldn't be cut, the computer would certainly report it. Let's try the hydraulics first. We're getting pressure in our brake cylinders here. The only way we can get that is if this valve is opened slightly – '

'Or if something is blocking it so it can't close completely.'

'Eino, you're reading my mind. And what could be blocking it is just plain dirt. The filter in the line here is supposed to be cleaned out after every trip. A nasty, dirty job crawling around under the cars. A job I remember assigning to a certain mechanic named Decio some years ago. A mechanic so bad that I eventually demoted him right back to the farm. When we stop we'll drop one of those filters and look at it.'

Eino rubbed his jaw with a calloused hand. 'If that's the trouble we are going to have to drain each malfunctioning brake system to get the valves out to clean.'

'No need. These emergency valves, here and here, shut tight if the line is broken. We won't lose much fluid. There are spare control valves in stock. What we'll do is replace the first valves with new ones, have the old valves cleaned while we are working and exchange them down the line. The gradients aren't too bad this first day, we'll leave the brakes cut out on the few cars with trouble.'

'Jan,' the co-driver called out. 'Mountains in sight so the tunnel will be coming up soon. Thought you would want the con.'

'Right. Leave the specs here, Eino, and get back to your engine. We'll be hitting the slope soon.'

Jan slid into the driver's seat and saw the sharp peaks of the mountains ahead, stretching away, unbroken, on both sides. This was the range that kept the interior of the continent a desert, holding all the storms and rain on the far side. Once through the range they would find weather again. The Road ahead began to rise as they entered the foothills. Jan kept the autopilot on steer, but released the other controls. As the slope grew steeper he let up on the accelerator and dropped into the central gear range. He could see the

Road rising up ahead and there, above, the dark mouth of a tunnel. He switched on his microphone.

'All drivers. The tunnel is coming up in a few minutes. Headlights on as soon as you spot it.'

He switched on his own lights as he said this and the Road ahead sprang into harsh clarity.

The engineers who had built the Road, centuries earlier, had almost unlimited energy at their disposal. They could raise islands from the ocean – or lower them beneath the surface, level mountains and melt solid rock. To them the easiest way to pass the mountain range was by boring straight through it. They were proud of this, too, for the only decoration or non-functioning bit of the entire Road was above the tunnel entrance. Jan saw it now, cut into the solid rock, as the dark mouth loomed closer. A one-hundred-metre high shield. The headlights caught it as the Road straightened for the final approach. A shield with a symbol on it that must be as ancient as mankind: a hand holding a short and solid hammer. This was clear, growing larger, until it swept by above and they were inside the tunnel.

Rough stone wall flashed by, grey and empty. Apart from the occasional stream of water that crossed the Road the tunnel was featureless. Jan watched his tachometer and speedometer and left the steering to the autopilot. Almost half an hour passed before a tiny light appeared ahead, grew to a disc, then a great burning doorway.

They had gone far enough south, and risen high enough, to have driven into the dawn.

The massive engine tore out of the tunnel and into searing sunlight. The windscreen darkened automatically at the actinic onslaught, opaquing completely before the sun. Beta Aurigae was blue-white and searingly hot, even at this northern latitude. Then it was obscured by clouds and a moment later dense rain crashed down on the train. Jan started the windscreen wipers and switched on his nose radar. The Road was empty ahead. As quickly as it had begun the storm was over and, as the Road wound down out of the mountains, he had his first view of the acid green jungle with the blue of the ocean beyond.

'That's quite a sight,' Jan said, hardly aware he had spoken aloud.

'It means trouble. I prefer the inland driving,' the co-driver Otakar said.

'You're a machine without a soul, Otakar. Doesn't all that twilit monotony get you down at times.'

'No.'

'Message from the forward Road crew,' Hyzo called out. 'They've got a problem.'

Otakar nodded gloomily. 'I told you, trouble.'

Chapter Six

'What's happening?' Jan said into the microphone.

'*Lajos here. No big problems clearing the Road until now. Earthquake, at least a couple of years ago. About a hundred metres of Road missing.*'

'Can't you fill it in?'

'*Negative. We can't even see the bottom.*'

'What about going around it?'

That's what we're trying to do. But it means blasting a new road out of the cliff. It's going to take at least a half a day.

Jan cursed silently to himself; this was not going to be an easy trip at all if it continued this way. 'Where are you?' he asked.

'*About a six-hour drive from the tunnel.*'

'We'll join you. Keep the work going. Out.'

Six hours. That would mean a shorter day than planned. But they had work to do on the brakes. And there were sure to be other problems as people settled down. Get the brakes fixed, get around the collapsed bit of Road and press on in the morning. Everyone could use a night's sleep.

The Road had dropped down from the mountain slopes to the coastal plain, and as it fell the landscape had changed completely. Gone were the rocky slopes and the occasional bush with a precarious roothold in the scree. It was jungle now, high, thick jungle that cut out all sight of the ocean and only permitted a narrow view of the sky. There was plenty of evidence here that the jungle was trying to retake the Road. Burned trees and vegetation were on both sides now, where they had been bulldozed aside by the tanks that had gone on ahead. There was animal life, too, dark forms glimpsed briefly in the shadows beside the Road. At one point a line of green flying creatures had floated slowly out of the jungle and across the Road. Two of them had smashed into the engine's windscreen, to slowly slide away leaving blue smears of blood behind. Jan washed away the traces with the touch of a button. The engine was back on autopilot and there was little to do except watch the tunnel of the Road open up ahead.

'Tired, Otakar?' he asked.

'A little. A night's sleep will help.'

'But tomorrow will be a long day and every day after that. Even if we spell each other at the wheel it's going to be hard because we won't be able to rest, not just changing places between driver and co-driver.' Jan had the beginnings of an idea and he worked at it. 'What we need are more co-drivers. For this engine and all the others. That way we could have an experienced driver at the wheel all the time and the one off duty can get his eyes shut.'

'There aren't any other drivers.'

'I know that, but we could train some as we go.'

Otakar grunted and shook his head. 'No way. Every man with a trace of technical ability is already on a job. Or like your ex-mechanic Decio – who is back on the farm where he belongs. I don't want any farmers in the driving compartment.'

'You're right – but only half right. What about training some women as drivers?' Jan smiled as Otakar's jaw dropped.

'But . . . women don't drive. Women are just women.'

'Only in this outpost of hell, my boy. Even on Earth the exams are strictly competitive and workers rise as high as their ability allows, irrespective of their sex. It makes sound economic sense. I see no reason why the same thing can't be done here. Find the girls with ability and train them for the job.'

'The Hradil is not going to like this, or any of the Family Heads.'

'Of course not – and what difference does it make? This is an emergency and we need emergency measures.' Mention of The Hradil brought a sweeter name to mind from the same family. He smiled at the thought. 'Have you ever noticed the embroidery that Alzbeta Mahrova does.'

'I have a piece, traded it from the family.'

'Well that takes patience, skill, concentration –'

'All the traits of a successful driver!' Otakar was smiling now too. 'This mad idea may work. It will sure make life a bit brighter during the drive.'

'I'm for that,' Hyzo's voice called out from the speaker: he had been listening on the intercom to the conversation. 'Wouldn't like to have me train a radio operator or two?'

'You might very well. Later. Right now we want to put together a list of the women we know who might have ability in this direction. But don't say a word outside of this compartment. I want to hit the Elders with this later when they are tired and off-balance.'

Night fell before they reached the break in the Road. They were climbing again and the rock wall rose up on their right, while to the left the Road ended only in blackness. Jan slowed the speed of the trains gradually as a blip appeared on the nose radar. When he caught a glimpse of metal ahead on the Road he cut the high beams of his lights and sent out the stop signal.

'Begin braking now.'

As his own train slowed he knew that, stretching far back into the night, the long column of trains was also reducing speed continually. As they slowed to a complete stop Otakar entered the time in his log, then began shutting down the engine for standby. Jan rose and stretched. He was tired – but knew the night's work was just beginning.

'987 kilometres today,' Otakar said, entering the figure in the log.

'That's fine.' Jan massaged the tired muscles in his legs. 'That leaves us only something like 26,000 more to go.'

'The longest journey begins with but a single turn of the wheel,' Eino said, popping up from the engine-room hatch.

'You can just keep your folk philosophy to yourself. Shut down the engine, put all systems on standby and start pulling that brake valve from car seven. By the time you get it out I'll bring you a replacement. And check the filter as well.'

Jan cracked the exit door and a wave of hot, moist air washed over him. The engines and the cars were completely air-conditioned and he had forgotten how much further south they were. He could feel the sweat already dampening his skin as he climbed down the rungs. Very soon now they would have to use the coldsuits when they went outside the trains. He walked the hundred metres towards the ragged cliff that marked the end of the road. Bright lights illuminated the work area and the roar and grind of the tanks echoed from the rocky wall, punctuated by the continuous explosions of the fusion guns. The flaming mouths of the tank-mounted units had already carved a niche into the sheer rock wall to span the gap of missing Road. Now they were working to deepen and widen it to permit the trains to pass. Jan didn't interfere, they were doing fine without him. And he had business with the Family Elders.

They met in the lead car of the Taekeng family, the largest available compartment. This family, the most conservative and inbred, still kept many of their customs from distant Earth. There were silk hangings on the walls, scenes of water and birds and other strange animals, as well as sentences in an alphabet none of them could read. They were also the most group-social family so did not have their living cars broken up into the many small compartments the others preferred. The normal occupants of the room had been dispossessed for the moment, but they did not seem to mind. They were gathered in the Road outside the car, calling excitedly to each other about the work ahead, the stars overhead, the strange smells from the jungle below. Children ran about and were called back with great excitement when they ventured too near the precipice. A baby wailed in the darkness then smacked contentedly as it was put to the breast. Jan picked his way through the people and entered the car.

Though he had called the meeting they had started without him. That was obvious. Hein Ritterspach stood before the Family Heads, but he stopped talking as Jan entered. He gave one look of intense hatred before he turned his back, holding the cast on his arm before him like a shield. Jan took one look at the circle of stony faces and knew perfectly well what Hein was trying to do. But it wouldn't work. He went slowly to an empty chair and dropped into it.

'As soon as Ritterspach leaves, this meeting can begin,' he said.

'No,' Chun Taekeng broke in. 'He has some grave charges that must be heard. He has said – '

'I don't care what he said. If you wish to hold a meeting of Family Heads to listen to him you may do it any time you choose. Tonight if you wish. After our business is finished. I have called this meeting as Trainmaster and we have urgent matters to discuss.'

'You can't throw me out!' Hein shouted. 'As Proctor Captain I have a right to attend.'

Jan sprang to his feet and put his face close to the other's ruddy one. 'You have the right to leave, nothing else, that is an order.'

'You cannot order *me*, you attacked me, there are charges . . .'

'You drew a gun on me, Hein, and I defended myself. There are witnesses. I will prefer charges when we reach Southtown. If you insist on bothering me now I shall arrest you now, for endangering the safety of the train, and I shall imprison you. Now go.'

Hein's eyes swept the room looking for some evidence of aid. Chun opened his mouth – then shut it. The Hradil sat as unmoving and expressionless as a snake. There was only silence. Hein choked out a sound and stumbled to the door, fumbling at the handle with his left hand then vanished into the night.

'Justice will be done in Southtown,' The Hradil said.

'It will be done,' Jan answered, his voice as expressionless as hers. 'After the trip. Now, are there any troubles I should know about?'

'There are complaints,' Ivan Semenov said.

'I don't want to hear them. Morale, complaints, food, personal problems, all of these will be handled by the Family Heads. I mean mechanical problems, air, power, anything like that?'

He looked from face to face, but there was no response. It had to continue this way. He had to keep them off balance, unable to adjust completely to this new mode of life.

'Good. I knew I could rely upon you all to make things smoother for the technical crew. There are other ways in which you can help. As you know we shall be driving for twice the normal amount each day. This is only the first day so fatigue is not showing yet. But it will. The drivers will be working double time so will soon be twice as tired as normal. We may have accidents which we *cannot* afford. Unless we train more drivers as we go.'

'Why do you bother us with this?' Chun Taekeng asked abrasively. 'This is a technical matter about which you boast great proficiency. With no farming to be done there are plenty of men to choose from, so choose who you will.'

'Begging your pardon, but I would not trust any of your horny handed field workers near my machinery. Every man with any technical skills or abilities is now working or training.'

'If you have them all, why do you come to us?' The Hradil asked.

'I said men. My drivers tell me that they know many women with the skills and reflexes we need. They could be trained . . .'

'Never!' The Hradil exploded the word, her eyes narrowed to slits buried in a webwork of ancient wrinkles. Jan turned to face her, the closest he had ever been before, and realized that her cap of snowy hair was really a wig. So she had vanity. Perhaps that knowledge could be turned to some good use.

'Why not?' he asked quietly.

'Why? You dare ask? Because a woman's place is in the home. With her children, the family, that is the way it always has been done before.'

'Well that's not the way it will be done in the future. The ships always come. They did not come. The ships take the corn. We are carrying the corn south. The ships bring the seed and supplies we need. There is no seed or supplies. Women do not do technical work. They do now. My co-driver tells me that Alzbeta Mahrova, of your family, does skilled and delicate embroidery. He feels a woman with those talents could be trained as a co-driver. Then he could relieve me as driver. You can send her there now.'

'*No!*'

There was silence then. Had he pushed too hard? Maybe, but he had to push to keep them off balance – while he kept his balance. He had to stay in command. The silence went on and on, then was suddenly broken.

'You pick on only one,' Bruno Becker said in his slow and solemn manner. 'The girls in the Becker family are as good at embroidery as the Mahrovas. Some say even better. My daughter-in-law, Arma, is known for the delicacy of her work.'

'I know it,' Jan said, turning his back on The Hradil, deliberately, smiling and nodding enthusiastically. 'And she is a very smart girl as well. A moment, yes, isn't her brother driver of nine train? I thought so. I'll have him send for her. Her own brother will be able to tell her worth and whether she will be able to be trained as a co-driver.'

'Her embroidery is like chicken droppings in the sand,' The Hradil spluttered.

'I'm sure both girls do fine work,' Jan said calmly. 'But that is not the question. It is whether they can be trained to do a co-pilot's work. I'm sure Otakar will be able to train Alzbeta as easily as Arma's brother can teach her.'

'Impossible. Alone, with only men.'

'A problem easily solved. Very sensible of you to remind me. When Alzbeta comes in the morning to the engine be sure a married woman is with her. You've solved in advance what might be a problem, Hradil, I do thank you. Now let us prepare a list of women who might be suitable for this work.'

There seemed to be no trouble. The Family Heads were suggesting names, drawing up lists, with Jan agreeing and writing down the ones they thought best. Only The Hradil was silent. Jan chanced a look at her expressionless face and realized that all her feelings were in her eyes; burning pits of hatred. She knew what he had done and was filled with arctic loathing, frozen by it. If she had disliked him before she hated him now, with a ferocity beyond belief. Jan turned away and tried to ignore her because he knew there was absolutely nothing he could do about it.

Chapter Seven

'Another hour at least,' Lajos Nagy said. 'We have to blast more headroom or the engines will never get through. And I want to do static tests on the outer lip. I don't like the condition of some of the rock.' He had been up an entire day and night, had worked right through the night. His skin was pale and marked by dark patches, like soot, under his eyes.

'How many tanks will it take?' Jan asked.

'Two. The ones with the oversize fusion guns.'

'Leave those two and start ahead with the rest of the tanks You must stay ahead of us.'

'I'll follow with these . . .'

'Oh no you won't. You look like hell, do you know that?' I want you asleep when the tanks leave. We've got a long trip ahead and a lot more trouble I'm sure. Now don't argue or I'll give your job back to Hein.'

'You've talked me into it. Now that you mention it I do feel like lying down.'

Jan walked slowly across the newly carved Road towards the waiting trains. He looked out at the harsh blue of the sky and winced at the glare. The sun was still behind the mountains but it would rise soon enough. Beyond the sharp edge of the cliff there were only clouds hiding the jungle below. It was going to be a hot day. And get still hotter. He turned back to his engine to see Eino leaning against the golden flank of metal sucking on a cold pipe. There was grease on his hands and arms and even on his face.

'All done,' he told told Jan. 'Took most of the night, but worth it. I'll doze in the engine-room. Didn't put the new

66

brake valves in, no need. Old ones just gummed up. Rinsed out and put back. Work fine. Changed the filters in the lines too. Solid with gunk. I'd like to bend that Decio over my knee. He never touched a one of them.'

'Maybe I'll let you do that. After the trip.'

The few hours' sleep he had grabbed had restored Jan and he enjoyed the climb up the side of the engine. As he clambered up the sun broke over the hills and shone on the metal so that, even through half-closed eyes, he was in the centre of a golden glare. Half-blinded he went through the hatch and slammed it after him. The air was cool and dry.

'Gear box temperature, tyre temperature, brake drum temperature, bearing temperature.'

It wasn't Otakar who was speaking, but a far sweeter and familiar voice. To think he had forgotten! Alzbeta sat in the co-driver's seat, with Otakar standing behind her nodding his head happily. Not two feet away sat a pudgy, grey-haired woman, knitting with grim ferocity. The Hradil's own daughter, watchdog and guardian of virgins. Jan smiled to himself as he slipped into his driver's chair. Alzbeta glanced up at the motion and her voice died.

'She's doing absolutely fantastic,' Otakar said. 'About ten times brighter and ten times smarter than the last dim dirt-scratcher I tried to teach this job to. If the other girls are anywhere as good, our driver problem is solved.'

'I'm sure they will be,' Jan said, but his eyes were on Alzbeta as he spoke. So close he could almost touch her. Those dark eyes looking deep into his.

'I like this work too,' she said. Very seriously, her back to the others. Only Jan could see her eyes move up and down his body, followed by the slow wink.

'For the good of the train,' he said, just as seriously. 'I am glad that this plan will work. Isn't that so, aunty?'

The Hradil's daughter returned only a glare of pure

67

malice before bending back to her knitting. She had been well briefed by her mother. Her presence could be suffered. It was small enough price to pay to have Alzbeta near by. When he spoke it was to Otakar – but his eyes were on the girl.

'How soon before you think she will be ready to spell you as co-driver?'

'Compared to some of the dumbies on these trains, I would say she is ready now. But let her have a day here at least, observing, then perhaps tomorrow she can try a trial run in the seat with me standing by.'

'Sounds good to me. What do you think, Alzbeta?'

'I'm . . . not sure. The responsibility.'

'The responsibility is not yours, it is the driver's. I or Otakar will be in this seat. Making the decisions and driving the train. Your job will be to help, to keep track of things, to watch the instruments, to follow orders. As long as you stay calm you can do it. Do you think you can?'

Her jaw was clamped tight and, beautiful as she was, there was more than a little of The Hradil in her when she spoke.

'Yes. I can do it. I *know* I can do it.'

'Very good. Then it is all arranged.'

When the fusion guns had finished cutting the new Road, Jan personally walked every foot of it, the exhausted tank operater plodding at his side. They walked along the lip, just a metre from the sheer fall into the jungle far below. Despite the breeze the cutting was like an oven, the rock still warm under their feet. Jan knelt and tapped the edge of the rock with a heavy ball pean hammer he carried. A chunk of stone broke away and rattled down the slope and vanished over the drop.

'I don't like some of this rock. I don't like it at all,' he said. The tank operator nodded.

'Don't like it myself. If we had more time I would widen

68

the cut. I've done what I can with melt compacting. Hope the lava flow on the surface will penetrate and hold it together.'

'You're not the only one to hope that. All right, you've done all you can now. Get your tanks through and I'll bring the first train over.' He started away, then turned back. 'You've dug in the guide wire as we planned?'

'Absolute minimum clearance. If it was one centimetre to the right you would be taking off the top of the engine.'

'Good.' Jan had been thinking about this and he knew what had to be done. There would be protests, but they would follow his orders. His own crew were predictably the first.

'You'll need an engineer for this job,' Eino said. 'I promise not to sleep.'

'I will not need one. The engines will be dead slow all the way so they can do without your attention for a few minutes. Nor will I need a co-driver or a communications officer for that short a time. Clear the driving compartment. Once we're past this you'll learn the job, Alzbeta.' He guided her towards the hatch with his hand on her elbow, ignoring the gasps and raised knitting needles of her chaperone. 'Don't worry.'

There were more protests from the passengers as they were unloaded but, in a few minutes, Jan was alone in the train. If anything happened he would be the only one to suffer. They could not afford to waste more time here; they must press on.

'All clear,' Otakar called from the open hatch. 'I can still come along.'

'See you on the other side. Clear the train, I'm starting.'

He touched lightly on the accelerator and, at absolutely minimum speed, the engine crawled forward. As soon as it was moving he set the autopilot and took his hands from the wheel. He was committed. The engine would take itself across in a far more controlled manner than he himself could. As the train crept forward he went to the open hatch and looked at the edge of the Road. If there were trouble, it would be there. Centimetre by centimetre they crawled through the newly burned section of Road, closer and closer to the far end.

The sound was a grinding rumble, easily heard above the drone of the engine, and as the noise began cracks appeared in the hard surface of the stone. Jan started to turn to the controls, then realized he could do nothing. He stood, his fingers tightclamped to the edge of the hatch as a great section of Road broke away and vanished with a roar towards the valley floor, far below. Cracks spread like deadly fingers across the surface, reaching for the train.

Then stopped.

There was a great gap now, a chunk bitten out of the solid rock of the Road. But it ended short of the engine. The powerful machine lumbered past the opening and Jan sprang back to the controls, frantically switching from camera to camera to get a view of the following car. Now the engine was through safely, past the gap.

However, the cars it pulled were almost three times wider.

His foot was a fraction of a centimetre above the brake pedal, his fingers resting on the autopilot, his eyes fixed on the screen.

The wheels of the first car crept towards the gap, the outer, double wheel, apparently aimed directly at it. It would never get past. He was about to stamp on the brakes when he looked closer. Just possibly.

The wheel rolled to the edge of the gap and dropped over the lip.

The outer tyre of the two. It turned slowly in the air, blue sky showing under it. All the weight of the overloaded car came on to the inner wheel.

As the tyre skirted the very edge of the drop it compressed under the weight, flattening to an oval. Then the other tyre hit the far edge of the gap and the car was safe on the other side. The radio bleeped in Jan's ear and he switched it on.

'Did you see *that*?' Otakar asked, in a very weak voice.

'I did. Stay close by and report on the broken area. I'm going to take the rest of the train across. If it stays this way it will be fine. But tell me *instantly* if there are any more falls.'

'I'll do that, you can be sure.'

At minimum crawling speed the cars followed, one by one, until the entire train was safely across the gap. As soon as the last car was reported safely past Jan killed the engine, jammed on the brakes – and let out a deep sigh. He felt as though every muscle in his body had been worked over with a heavy hammer. To relieve the tension he jogged back to the new section of Road to join Otakar.

'No more falls, none at all,' the co-driver reported.

'Then we should be able to get the other trains through.' The passengers were crossing on foot now, pressed as close to the inside walls as they could, looking with frightened eyes at the cliff edge and the gaping crevice. 'Take the first engine and keep going. Half speed until all the trains are over. It should go well now. When they are through I'll catch up on the cycle. Any questions?'

'Nothing I can put into words. This is your show, Jan. Good luck.'

It was hours before the last train was past, but they all made it safely. There were no more rock falls. As Jan sped along beside the slow moving trains he wondered what the next emergency would be.

Happily, it was a long time coming. The Road crossed the coastal ranges and cut across the alluvial coastal plain that fringed the continent. This was an almost entirely flat and featureless swamp, formerly the coastal banks, shoal water, lifted up by the engineers. The Road was on a raised dyke for the most part, cutting straight as a ruled line through the reeds and tree-grown tussocks. All that the maintenance tanks had to do, for the most part, was burn off intruding vegetable life and repair the occasional crack caused by sub-sidence. They moved faster than the heavy-laden trains and were drawing further and further ahead, making up most of the two-day lead they had lost. The nights had been growing shorter until the day when the sun did not set at all. It dropped to the southern horizon, a burning blue ball of fire, then moved into the sky again soon afterwards. After this it was always above their heads, its intensity increasing as they headed south. The temperature outside had been rising steadily and now stood at well over 150 degrees. When there had still been a night many people had emerged from the cramped, boring quarters to move about on the Road des-pite the breathless heat. With the sun now in the sky con-stantly this could not be done and morale was being strained to the breaking point. And there were still 18,000 kilometres to go.

They were driving a full nineteen hours every day now and the new co-drivers were proving their worth. There had been some grumbling among the men at first about women out of their natural place, but this had stopped as fatigue had taken over. The extra help was needed. Some of the women had not been able to learn the work, or had not the stamina for it, but there were more than enough new volun-teers to take their places.

Jan was happier than he remembered for years. The fat chaperone had complained about the climb up to the driving compartment and, when the heat had increased, it had been impossible to find a coldsuit big enough for her. A married cousin of Alzbeta's had taken the watchdog role for one day, but said she was bored by it and had her children to

72

take care of and refused to come back the following day. Her absence had not been reported at once to The Hradil and by the time she had learned about it the damage – or lack of damage – had been done. Alzbeta had survived a day alone with three men and was none the worse for the experience. By unspoken agreement the chaperone's role was dropped.

Alzbeta sat in the co-driver's seat while Jan drove. Otakar would sleep on the cot in the engine-room, or play cards with Eino. Hyzo found it easy to get permission to join the games, Jan cheerfully stood radio watch for him, and though the hatch behind them was open Jan and Alzbeta were alone for the first time since they had met.

At the very first it was embarrassing. Not for Jan. It was Alzbeta who would blush and hang her head when he talked and forgot her job as co-driver. Her lifetime of training was fighting her intelligence. Jan ignored this for one shift, not even making small talk, thinking she would be over it by the second day. When she was not he lost his temper.

'I've asked you for that reading twice now. That's too much. You are here to aid me, not make my job more difficult.'

'I – I'm sorry. I'll try not to do it again.'

She lowered her head and blushed even more and Jan felt like a swine. Which he was. You don't break the conditioning of years in a moment. The Road was clear ahead and dead straight, nothing on the nose radar. The trains rolled at a steady 110 kilometres per hour and the wheel could be left unattended, for perhaps a moment. He rose and went to Alzbeta and stood behind her, his hands resting lightly on her shoulders. Like a frightened animal's, her body quivered beneath his touch.

'I'm the one who should be sorry,' he said. 'I'll drag Hyzo

73

away from the poker game, it's time for a driver check in any case.'

'No, not yet. It is not that I don't like being alone with you, it's the other way round. I have known that I have loved you for a very long time, but only now am I finding out what that really means.'

She put her hands up to her shoulders to cover his, turned her face to look up at him. When he bent his head to kiss her, her mouth came up to meet his. When his hands slid down to cup her full breasts her hands held them tight, pulling him to her. It was he who broke away first, knowing this was neither the time nor the place.

'See, The Hradil was right,' he said, trying to make light of it.

'No! She was wrong in every way. She will not keep us apart and I will marry you. She cannot stop . . .'

The flashing red light on the radio console and the rapid beeping sent him leaping to the driver's chair, thumbing on the radio. Behind him Hyzo shot up from the engine-room as though he had been propelled from a cannon.

'Trainmaster here.'

'*Jan, Lajos here with the tanks. We've hit something too big to handle. It looks like we've lost one tank, though no one injured.*'

'What is it?'

'*Water, just water. The Road's gone. I can't describe it, you'll have to see for yourself.*'

There were complaints, but Jan kept the trains rolling until they caught up with the maintenance tanks. He was asleep when they picked up the first blip on the nose radar. He awoke at once and slid into the driver's seat as Otakar vacated it.

As it had for days, the Road still traversed the coastal swamps. Continually different, yet always the same, the haze

74

shrouded wastes of reed and water had been changing imperceptibly. The ratio of open water to swamp was growing until, most suddenly, the swamps were gone and there was only water on both sides of the causeway. Jan slowed the train and the others behind automatically followed. First the radar picked out the individual specks of the vehicles, then he could make them out by sight.

It was frightening. The Road dropped lower and lower above the surrounding water until, a little past the tanks, it vanished completely. Beyond them there was just water, no sign of the Road at all. Just a calm ocean stretching away on all sides.

Jan shouted to Otakar to finish the shut down procedures since, the instant the brakes were set, he was at the exit hatch, pulling on a coldsuit. Lajos was waiting below when he dropped on to the Road.

'We've no idea how far it goes,' he said. 'I tried to get across with a tank, you can see the turret of it about two kilometres out. It's deeper there, flooded me suddenly. I just had time to hit the dampers and get out. The next tank threw me a rope, pulled me free.'

'What happened?'

'Just a guess. It looks like there was a general subsidence of the land here. Since it was all under water once maybe it's just dropping back where it came from.'

'Any idea how wide this thing is?'

'None. Radar won't reach and the telescopes just show more haze. It may end in a few kilometres. Or go on until it drops down to the ocean bottom.'

'You're optimistic.'

'I was in that water – and it's hot. And I can't swim.'

'Sorry. I'll go take a look myself.'

'The Road cable is still in place. You can't see anything but the instruments can track it.'

Jan clumped round to the rear of the engine, his movements hampered by the thick coldsuit. The suit was lined with a network of tubes filled with cold water. A compact refrigeration unit on his belt hummed industriously and expelled the heated exhaust air to the rear. Cooled air was also blown across his face under the transparent helmet. The suit was tiring to wear after a few hours – but it made life possible. The outside air temperature now stood near 180 degrees. Jan switched on the built-in intercom at the rear of the engine.

'Otakar, can you hear me?'

'*Green.*'

'Set the interlocks to the cars, then disconnect the engine coupling. I'll disconnect the cables back here.'

'*Are we going for a ride?*'

'You might say that.'

There was a whirr and a clatter as the metal jaws of the coupling slowly opened. Jan pushed the heavy tongue aside, then unplugged all the cable connectors. There were loud thuds under the car behind him as the beta safety brakes were actuated. The cables retracted like snakes into a hole and he climbed back up to the driving compartment.

'I need three volunteers,' he told the waiting crew members as he pulled off the coldsuit. 'You, you and you. Alzbeta, take this suit and get back into the train. What we have to do may take awhile.'

She did not protest, but her eyes were on him as she pulled on the suit slowly and left. Otakar dogged the hatch shut after her. Jan studied the glimmering expanse of water ahead. 'Eino,' he said, 'just how waterproof are we?'

The engineer did not answer at once. He scratched at his ear in thought as he looked around slowly, looking through the steel walls and floor with a mechanic's eye, seeing all the joints, seals and hatches.

'Not bad at all,' he said, finally. 'We're made for a certain amount of water, drive trains and bearings, access ports and hatches all with gaskets. Higher up, all right too, at least for a while. I really think we could submerge right up to the roof without getting into trouble. Higher than that and we could short out the cooling fins on top. Up that far I would say we're waterproof.'

'Then I think we had better go before we change our minds.' He dropped into the driver's chair. 'Get on the engine – I may need a lot of power. Hyzo, keep the radio open and keep a report going back. If there is any trouble I want the others to know what happened. Otakar, stand by if I need you.'

'Going for a swim?' the co-driver asked calmly, flipping on switches.

'I hope not. But we have to find out if the Road is still there. We can't turn back and we can't stay here. And this is the only Road. This engine stands more than twice as high as the tank. It all depends on the depth of the water. Power.'

'Full.'

The tanks scuttled aside as the hulking engine ground forward. Straight towards the water until the front wheels sent out the first ripples. Then straight in.

'It's like being in a ship . . .' Otakar said, almost under his breath. *With the slight difference*, Jan thought, *that this engine doesn't float*. He did not say it aloud.

All about them was water of unknown depth. They knew the Road was still beneath them for the water had not yet reached the hubs of the great wheels. And the cable blip was high and centred, being followed automatically. But a bow wave was pushed up by the moving engine and they could have been in a ship for all the apparent connection they had with land – or even with the Road now falling back behind them.

The turret of the tank ahead was a solid reference point that they approached cautiously. As they came close the water rose steadily. Jan stopped a good twenty metres from the drowned vehicle.

'Water doesn't quite cover our wheels yet, plenty to go,' Otakar said, looking out of the side window. He tried to speak calmly but his voice was strained.

'How wide would you say the Road is here?' Jan asked.

'One hundred metres, as always, like the rest of the Road.'

'Is it? You don't think this water may have undercut it?'

'I hadn't thought . . .'

'I had. We'll go round the tank, as close as we can. And hope that it is solid enough under the wheels.'

He flipped off the autopilot as he spoke and turned the wheel slowly as they moved forward under complete manual. The high white blip of the central cable drifted across the screen until it vanished. It had been their only guide. Higher and still higher the water rose.

'I hope you're staying close to the tank,' Hyzo called out. He may have meant it as a joke. It had not sounded like one.

Jan tried to remember just how big the tank was under the water. He wanted to remain as near to it as possible without running into it. Passing as close as he could. Water, nothing but water on all sides, the only sound the rumble of the engines and drive and the hoarse breathing of the men.

'I can't see it any more,' Jan called out suddenly. 'Cameras are dead. Otakar!'

The co-driver had already jumped to the rear window.

'Easy on, almost past, falling slightly behind, you can turn sharp . . . now?'

Jan obeyed blindly. He could do nothing else. He was in the midst of an ocean, turning a wheel, with no reference marks at all. Not too much, straight, he should be past it now. Or was he going in the wrong direction? He would be off the edge of the Road soon. He was unaware of the sweat standing out on his face and dampening his palms.

The tiniest of blips on the cable screen.

'I have it again!'

He centred the wheel, then turned it gradually as the blip slowly moved across the screen to align itself. When it did so he flipped on the autopilot and leaned back.

'So much for that, now let's see how far this goes on.'

He kept the speed controls to himself but allowed the autopilot to track the cable. The Road was still beneath them, impossible as it seemed. They watched as a rainstorm blew towards them and washed over the engine, blanketing vision in all directions. Jan turned on the wipers and the headlights. There was a clatter of relays from the engine-room.

'You've lost about half your lights,' Eino reported. 'Shorted out, circuit breakers kicked out.'

'Will it mean trouble? What about the rest of the lights?'

'Should be all right. All the circuits are isolated.'

They went on. Rain on all sides and just the spattered surface of the water ahead. Water that rose higher and higher, slowly and surely. There was a sudden ascending whine from the engine-room and the engine shuddered, lurching sideways.

'What is it?' Hyzo called out, an edge of panic in his voice.

'Revs up,' Jan said, clinging to the wheel, turning it, trying to follow the blip of the cable that was sliding off the screen, killing the autopilot as he did. 'But Road speed down. We're moving sideways.'

'Sand – or mud on the Road!' Otakar shouted. 'We're slipping.'

'And we're losing the cable.' Jan turned the wheel even

more. 'This thing is almost afloat, the wheels are not getting the traction they should. But they will.'

He stamped hard on the accelerator and the transmission roared deeply from below. The drive wheels spun in the mud, churning it up, digging into it, roiling the surface of the water around them. The sliding still continued – the cable blip was gone from the screen.

'We'll go off the edge!' Hyzo shouted.

'Not yet.' Jan's teeth almost met in the flesh of his lip, but he was not aware of it.

There was a lurch, then another one as the wheels touched the surface of the Road. He cut the power as they gripped again, then crept forward. Moment after moment of silence. Until the cable blip appeared again. He centred it, and looked at the compass to make sure they were not going in the opposite direction. The engine crawled ahead. The rain passed and he killed the lights.

'I'm not sure . . . but I think the water is lower,' Otakar said in a hoarse voice. 'Yes, it is, it must be, that rung was under water a minute ago.'

'I'll tell you something even better,' Jan said, cutting in the autopilot and dropping back heavily in the chair. 'If you look directly ahead I think you'll see where the Road comes out of the water again.'

The level of the water sank until the wheels were clear, throwing spray in all directions then they were up on the solid surface once more and Jan killed the power and set the brakes.

'We're across. The Road is still there.'

'But – can the trains make it?' Otakar asked.

'They are going to have to, aren't they?'

There was no answer to that.

Chapter Eight

Before there could be any thought of taking the trains across the drowned section of Road, there was the barricade of the abandoned tank to be considered. Jan drove the engine back down the Road, with scarcely any trouble passing the mud-coated section on the return trip, and stopped a few metres from the tank.

'Any ideas?' he asked.

'Any chance of starting it up?' Otakar asked.

'Negative. The pile has been damped and all the circuits are wet by now. But there is something we have to find out before we even look for a way to tackle this.' He put in a call to Lajos, who had been driving the tank when it went under. The answer was not cheering at all. 'The drive is still engaged. About the only thing we can do with that tank is push it aside. And we can't do that unless it will roll free. It will be impossible to skid that amount of dead weight.'

'You're the Maintenance Captain,' Otakar said. 'So you are the one to answer that question best.'

'I know the answer. With the power dead, the manual disengage lever has to be used. But the trouble is that the thing is clamped to the inside rear wall. It has to be unhooked, fitted into place, then turned about a dozen times. All of this under – what? – about three metres of water. Do you swim, Otakar?'

'Where would I learn to do that?'

'A good question. Too much fertilizer in the canal to swim there – and that is the only body of water near the city. You think someone would have planned a swimming pool

81

when the cities were designed. It wouldn't have taken much. I imagine that leaves me as the only swimmer on Halvmörk. A reluctant volunteer. But I'll need some help.'

There was no easy way to make a face mask, but one of the pressure bottles filled with compressed air was simple enough to arrange. Jan worked with the valve until it released a steady flow of air, smelling of oil and grease, that should supply his needs without blowing his head off. Eino arranged a sling so he could carry it at his waist, with a plastic tube to his mouth. That and a waterproof light were all he needed.

'Bring us as close as you can,' he told Otakar as he stripped off his clothes. He kept his boots on. The metal would be hot, and he would need gloves as well. When the two machines were touching, nose to nose, he cracked the top hatch. A wave of burning air rolled in. Without a word he climbed to the hatch and pushed it open.

It was like climbing into a baker's oven. The cool air of the engine was left behind in an instant as he emerged into the blinding, burning sunshine. He covered his eyes with his arm and shuffled the length of the engine's roof, picking his way between the cooling fins. Trying not to gasp in the hot air, forcing himself to suck the cooler air from the tube instead. Though the soles of his shoes were thick the heat of the metal was penetrating already. At the edge he did not hesitate, but eased himself over into the water.

It was a steaming cauldron that drained the energy from his body. One, two, three, strokes took him to the open hatch on the tank and he did not permit himself to hesitate but sank instantly beneath the surface. It was dark, too dark – then he remembered the light. The heat of the water about him was all-engulfing, draining both his will and energy. Now the lever, he must get it.

Everything moved as slowly as in a dream, and if his chest

hadn't hurt he thought he might go to sleep. He was getting air from the tank, but not enough. The lever. It came free easily enough, but fitting it over the stud seemed immensely difficult. When it finally clicked into place he lost precious seconds trying to remember which way to move it. Then the turns, over and over until it would turn no more.

Time. Time to go. The lever and the torch dropped from his fingers and he tried to rise. But he could not. The light of the open hatch was clear above but he did not have the strength to swim up to it. With a last burst of his waning energy he tore the weight of the air tank away, spitting out the tube, and bent his knees. One last time. Pushing upwards, swimming upwards, hard, harder.

His hands came out of the water and clutched the edge of the hatch. Then his head was above the surface and he sucked in great gasps of the burning air. It hurt, but it cleared his head. When he was able, he dragged himself up and staggered across the top of the tank and threw himself in the direction of the engine.

And knew he could not make it, could not swim another stroke.

The rope splashed into the water beside his head and he clutched it reflexively. He was pulled to the engine, to the side, and Otakar reached down and took him by the wrists and pulled him from the water like an expiring fish. Jan was barely aware of this, his consciousness fading in a red haze, until his leg brushed the metal of the engine's roof. Searing the flesh almost to the bone. He shouted aloud at the sudden pain, his eyes wide, aware that Otakar was helping him. Otakar without a coldsuit, gasping with exhaustion.

They leaned one on the other, as they made their way carefully across the top of the engine. Jan went down first, helped by the co-driver, who followed behind him. The air inside was arctic. For a long time all they could do was sit where they had dropped on the floor, fighting to recover.

'Let us not do that again if we can avoid it,' Jan said, finally. Otakar could only nod weak agreement.

Hyzo put burn cream on Jan's leg, then wrapped it in gauze. It was painful, but a pill took care of that. And his fatigue as well. Dressed again, he sat in the driver's chair and checked his controls.

'Any sign of leaking yet?' he asked the engineer.

'Negative. This beast is tight.'

'Good. Give me plenty of power. I'm going to push that tank off the Road. What will I break if I push it nose to nose?'

'Couple of lights, nothing important. We have solid steel there, four centimetres thick. Weight for traction. Just push.'

Jan did. Easing forward at slowest possible revs until metal ground against metal and the engine shuddered. Keeping in the lowest gear he pressed down steadily on the accelerator. The clutches growled deeply and the entire engine shuddered as it fought against the dead weight of the tank. Something had to give.

The tank moved. Once it had started to roll backwards Jan kept the speed steady and turned the wheel ever so slightly, centring it again to hold the gradual turn. Bit by bit they turned until they left the cable behind and the tank was pointing at right angles to the Road. Jan centred the wheel and went on. Further and further from the centre. Closer and closer to the edge.

Suddenly the tank reared up and Jan hit the brakes. It dropped over the edge instantly and, from the angle, the engine was just at the edge itself. Slowly and carefully he put the engine in reverse and backed away from the danger. Only when they were lined up again in the centre of the Road did he let the air out of his lungs with a deep sigh.

'I agree,' Otakar said. 'I hope this is the last of the trouble here.'

It was not easy, but there were no major problems in bringing the trains across the drowned stretch of Road. Just time. Wasted time. The cars, far lighter than the massive engines, had a tendency to float in the water. Two were the most that could be taken through at one time, and this possible only with an engine at either end. The shuttle continued without stop until all the cars were across. Only when the trains had been assembled on the far side of the drowned section did Jan permit himself to relax, to sleep for more than a few hours at a time. He had ordered an eight-hour rest period before they continued. Everyone needed it, the engine crews were exhausted, and he knew better than to press on with the drivers in this condition. They could rest but he could not. During the entire operation of moving the trains across the drowned section of Road he had been worrying away at a problem that refused to be dismissed. An obvious problem that faced him squarely when he drove back over the water-covered Road to the squadron of solitary tanks. He stopped the water-streaming engine next to the tanks, pulled on a coldsuit, and transferred to the lead tank.

'I thought you had forgotten about us,' Lajos Nagy said.

'Quite the opposite. I've been thinking of nothing else for days.'

'You going to leave the tanks here?'

'No – we need them too much.'

'But we can't cross under our own power.'

'I don't expect you to. Look at this.'

Jan unrolled a blueprint, a side projection of one of the tanks. He had marked it up liberally with a large red pen. He tapped the lines he had added.

'These are our problem areas,' he said. 'We are going to spray them all with mothball sealant. So they should be watertight long enough to get through the water and out on the other side.'

'Wait a bit,' Lajos said, pointing to the diagram. 'You've got all the exit hatches sealed shut. How can the driver get out if he has to?'

'No drivers. We take the treads out of gear, seal the tanks watertight – then tow them across. A single cable will do for each. I tried it and it works.'

'I hope so,' Lajos said, dubiously. 'But I would hate to be in the engine towing one of these things if it went off the edge of the Road. It will pull the engine over with it.'

'It might very well. That is why we are going to rig a tow release that can be operated from inside the engine. If the tank starts to go we just cut it loose.'

Lajos shook his head. 'I suppose there's nothing else for it. Let's try it with number six tank first. The clutches are almost shot and we may have to leave it behind in any case.'

There was a unanimous sigh of relief when the plan worked. The towed tank vanished beneath the water and wasn't seen again until it emerged on the other side of the sunken section of Road. The sealant was quickly scraped away and, except for a few puddles from a small leak, the tank was intact. The transfer of all the others began.

When the trek was ready to begin again the relief co-drivers were brought back to the engines. Alzbeta was carrying a sealed bundle that she set down when she took off her coldsuit.

'Something special,' she said. 'I made it myself. It is a family recipe for special occasions. I think this is a special occasion. Beef stroganoff.'

It was delicious. The crew sat down to the first meal they had enjoyed since the trek had begun. There was freshly baked bread with it, litres of beer and fresh green onions. There was even some cheese to follow though few, if any, had space for this. But they groaned heroically and made room for it.

'Our thanks,' Jan said, taking her hand despite the presence of others. No one complained, apparently no one even noticed. They accepted Alzbeta as part of the crew now. An improved part since no one else could do a thing about meals other than heat frozen concentrates. Jan had a sudden inspiration.

'We'll be rolling in about half an hour. That's just about time to check you out in the driver's seat, Alzbeta. You don't want to just be a co-driver all your life.'

'Good idea,' Otakar said.

'Oh, no, I couldn't. It's just not possible . . .'

'That's an order, see that you obey it.' His smile softened the impact of his words, and a moment later they were all laughing. Hyzo went for a rag and polished the chair for her, Otakar led her there and adjusted the seat so that she could reach the pedals easily. With the power off she tentatively stepped on the brakes and accelerator and tugged on the steering wheel. She already knew the function of all the instruments.

'See how simple it is,' Jan said. 'Now put it in reverse and back a few feet.' She went pale.

'That's different. I wouldn't be able to.'

'Why not?'

'You understand, it's your work.'

'For men only, you mean?'

'Yes, perhaps I do.'

'Then try it. You have been doing men-only work for the past week, you and the other girls, and the world hasn't come to an end.'

'Yes – I will!'

She said it defiantly – and meant it. Things were changing and she liked the changes. Without a word of instruction she turned on the engine, disconnected the autopilot and did all the other things needed to ready the engine. Then, ever so tentatively, she engaged the reverse gear and backed the engine a bit. Then, when she had shut down the engine again, everyone cheered.

When the trek began again they were all in the best of moods, rested and happy. Which was a good thing since the worst part of the journey was to come. The engineers who had built the Road had done their best to avoid all the natural hazards of the planet. As much as possible of the Road stayed behind the coastal mountain barriers of the two continents. The penetration of the mountains themselves was done by tunnel. The coasts were avoided for the most part by putting the Road on the dykes offshore. On the raised chain of islands, the isthmus that connected the two continents, the Road ran high along the spine of the islands, the high mountain ridges.

But there was one hazard that could not be avoided. Eventually the Road would have to cross the tropical jungle barrier. The southernmost part of the continent was eternal burning summer. With the air temperature just a few degrees below the boiling point of water, this was a jungle hell.

The Road turned back inland briefly, plunging through a mountain range. The tanks were thirty hours ahead and working on clearing the Road, so Jan had reports on the conditions. But, as always, the reality was beyond description. The tunnel fell at a steep angle and his headlights glared against rock and Road. There were letters here, etched eternally into the surface of the Road itself, SLOW they read, SLOW, repeated again and again. The tyres rumbled as they crossed the pattern of letters. As the glaring mouth of the tunnel appeared ahead the trains were doing a lumbering fifty kilometres an hour.

Trees, vines, plants, leaves, the jungle burst with life on all sides, above, even on the Road itself. The Road was over

200 metres wide here, twice its normal width, and still the jungle had overriden it as the burgeoning plant life fought for the light of the sun. In the four years since they had passed last, the trees on either side had sent long branches out, questing for the light. Often these had grown so large that they had overweighed and toppled the parent trees on to the Road. Some had died, and been used as a base for other plants and vines, while others, with their roots still fixed in the jungle, had thrived and grown higher from their new positions. Where trees had not obstructed the Road, creepers and vines, some a metre thick and more, had crawled out on to the sunny surface.

The tanks had joined in battle against the trees; the black remains of their victories lined the Road on both sides. With their flame-exploding snouts, the fusion guns had gone first, burning every obstruction before them. Then dozer blades had cleared a path just wide enough for their treads: the tanks that followed had widened this, pushing back the charred remains. Now the trains moved slowly between two walls of blackened debris, still smoking in places. It was a nightmare sight.

'It's horrible,' Alzbeta said. 'Horrible to look at.'

'I don't mean to make light of it,' Jan told her, 'but this is just the beginning. The worse part is up ahead. Of course it is dangerous out there, always, even when the trip is made at the usual time. And we are late this year, very late.'

'Will that make a difference?' she asked.

'I'm not sure – but if there is going to be any difference it will be for the worse. If only better records had been kept. I can't find anything at all from any early planetary surveys. All the memory tapes have been wiped clean. Of course there are logs of all the trips, but they aren't very helpful. Technical notes and mileages for the most part. But no personal journals of any kind. I suppose when everything has to be packed to be moved every couple of years odd items usually get thrown out. So I have no hard facts – just a feeling. It's spring that's bothering me.'

'I do not know the word.'

'Not in the language. No referrent. On more reasonable planets there are four seasons in the temperate zones. Winter is the cold time, summer is the hot. The time in between when everything is warming up, that's spring.'

Alzbeta shook her head and smiled. 'It is a little hard to understand.'

'There is something a little bit like it on this planet. At the edge of the twilight zone there are life forms that have adapted to the cooler environment. They have their ecological niche there and manage fine until summer returns. When it does all this burgeoning hot-zone life will probably rush in and make a meal of the cooler-adapted forms. The rule out there is eat and be eaten, so the competition for a new food source must be fierce.'

'But you can't be sure . . .'

'I'm not sure – and I also hope that I am wrong about it. Just cross your fingers and hope that our luck holds out.'

It didn't. At first the change seemed innocent enough, just a little incidental traffic slaughter of no real importance. Only Alzbeta seemed put out by it.

'The animals, they don't seem to know about machines. They just come out on to the Road and are run over, crushed.'

'There's nothing we can do about it. Don't look if it bothers you.'

'I must look. That is part of my job. But those little greenish things with the orange bands, there seem to be a lot of them, coming out of the jungle.'

Jan noticed them now, first individuals, then groups, more and more of them. They were like obscene parodies of terrestrial frogs that had grown as big as cats. A ripple of movement seemed to go over them as they advanced with a jerking, hopping motion.

'A migration, maybe,' he said. 'Or perhaps they are being chased by something. It's messy – but they can't hurt us.'

Or can they? As he spoke the words Jan felt a sudden disquiet. The edge of a memory. What was it? But any doubts at all called for caution. He switched off the speed control and let off on the accelerator, then turned on the microphone.

'Leader to all trains. Decrease speed by 20 K's *now*!'

'What's wrong?' Alzbeta asked.

The Road was becoming almost invisible, covered by the creatures that thronged across it, oblivious of the deadly wheels rushing towards them.

'Of course!' Jan shouted into the microphone. 'All drivers stop, *stop*. But don't use your brakes. Ease off on the power, power down to zero but watch your coupling pressure gauges or you'll jackknife. Repeat. Slow without braking, watch your coupling pressure, watch your nose radar for the train ahead of you.'

'What's happening? What's wrong?' Eino called in from the engine compartment.

'Animals of some kind, covering the Road, thousands of them, we're running them down, crushing them . . .'

Jan broke off as the engine lurched sideways, then he lashed out his hand to cut off the automatic steering and clutched at the steering wheel.

'It's like driving on ice . . . no friction . . . the wheels are beginning to slide on the bodies.'

And the cars were beginning to go too. In the monitor screens Jan saw that the whole train was beginning to wriggle like a snake as the cars skidded and the steering computer fought to keep them following in a straight line.

'Get the computer out of your steering circuits,' Jan ordered the other drivers, throwing the switch himself at the same time. A touch of power pulled ahead on the train and stopped the weaving for the moment. He dropped the speed again, slowly, slowly, plunging on into the solid wall of bodies.

'Jan, look ahead!'

Alzbeta's cry alerted him and he saw that the Road, straight until now, began to curve ahead in a shallow bend. An easy curve – normally. But what would happen now with the road surface as slick as oil?

The speed was dropping – but not fast enough. They were down to fifty and still dropping. And the curve began.

Jan still had the steering on manual, but he had to switch the computer back on so the cars of the train would track correctly behind him. A touch of the wheel, then centre it. The shallowest curve he could make, starting from the inside of the bend and drifting slowly to the outside. Half-way through now, almost to the edge. Speed down to forty ... thirty-five. A bit more on wheel. Going all right. If he could hold it there.

A quick look at the screens showed the cars snaking slightly, but following in his course. Almost through. There was a sudden bumping as they ran over the charred tree limbs where the tanks had cleared the surface. Good. This would add some friction. Just beyond the edge of the Road was the jungle, a sharp bank and what looked like water or swamp.

'The creatures on the Road, there seem to be less of them,' Alzbeta said. 'They're coming in groups now, fewer of them.'

'I hope you're right.' Jan felt, for the first time, the soreness in his hands where he had grappled the steering wheel.

'Doing ten K's now, cars tracking well.'

'*I can't hold it!*'

The words burst from the speaker, a cry of despair.

'Who are you? Identify!' Jan shouted into the mike.

'*Train two . . . jackknifing . . . have full brakes, still sliding . . . the EDGE!*'

Jan eased his own train to a stop, automatically, scarcely aware, listening to the scream of pain. The crashing, breaking sounds. Then silence.

'All trains stop,' Jan ordered. 'Report only if you are in trouble. Report.'

There was the hiss of static, nothing else.

'Train two, can you hear me? Come in two, report.' Just silence. Nothing. 'Train three, are you stopped?' This time there was an answer.

'*Three here. Stopped okay. No problems. Creatures still crossing the Road. There's a great trail of crushed bodies and blood ahead . . .*'

'That's enough, three. Start up, minimum speed ahead. Report as soon as you have train two in sight.' Jan flicked the switch to internal. 'Hyzo, can you raise train two at all?'

'*I'm trying,*' the communications officer answered. '*No signal from the engine. Chun Taekeng has his own radio on the train but he's not answering.*'

'Keep trying . . .'

'*Hold it. A signal here, I'll put it on . . .*'

The voice was gasping, frightened. '*. . . what happened. People hurt when we stopped. Send the doctor . . .*'

'This is the Trainmaster. Who is speaking?'

'*Jan? Lee Ciou here. We had a panic stop and people are hurt . . .*'

'More important, Lee. Are you still airtight – and is the air conditioning working?'

'*As far as I know. And I hope we're not holed because the*' *ground outside is covered with creatures of some kind. They're crawling over the cars, the windows.'*

'They can't hurt you as long as they can't get in. Get a report from the other cars and get back to me as soon as you can. Over and out.'

Jan sat stiffly, locked in concentration, staring unseeingly at the front port, his fist tapping heavily on the steering wheel. The train jackknifed – but power still on. So the engine generator must still be functioning. If so – then why couldn't they contact the crew? What had taken the radio out of circuit? He couldn't imagine what could have happened, but one thing was certain, he would need help to straighten out the mess. And he had already wasted precious minutes not calling for it.

'Hyzo,' he shouted into the intercom. 'Contact the tanks now. Tell them we've had train trouble and we will probably need some muscle to get out of it. I want the two biggest tanks with plenty of cable. Get them started back his way now at top speed.'

'Done. I've got train three on the circuit.'

'Put them through.'

'I have train two in sight ahead. Cars all over the Road, some even into the jungle. I've stopped now, just behind the last car.'

'Can you see the engine?'

'Negative.'

'Any chance of your getting by with your train?'

'Absolutely none. This thing is a mess! I've never seen . . .'

'Over and out.'

Hyzo, the communications officer, came on to the circuit as soon as Jan had killed it.

'I've got Lee Ciou in train two back on. Here he is.'

'Jan, can you hear me? Jan . . .'

'What did you find out, Lee?'

'*I've talked to the other car. They're shouting a lot and don't make sense, but I don't think anyone's dead. Yet. The car has some broken windows, but Chun Taekeng is taking over evacuation to this car. More important, I've got through to the engineer on the internal phone circuit.*'

'Did he tell you what's wrong?'

'*It's very bad. I've patched you through to him on the circuit.*'

'All right. Vilho, are you there? Vilho Heikki, come in.'

The radio sputtered and crackled and a distant voice was audible through the static.

'*Jan ... there's been a crackup. I was in the engine-room when we started sliding all over the Road. I heard Turtu shouting something – then we hit. Something real solid. Then the water, and Arma ...*'

'Vilho, I'm losing you. Can you talk louder?'

'*Real bad crackup. I started up the ladder when I saw the water. It was coming through the hatch. Maybe I should have got them out. But they didn't answer ... the water was coming in. So I slammed and sealed the hatch lid ...*'

'You did the right thing. You had the rest of the train to think about.'

'*Yes, I know ... but Arma Nevalainen ... she was co-driver.*'

There was no time for Jan to think about it. That his plan for the women to help drive had just killed one of them. He must think only of the others still in danger aboard the train.

'Are you holding power, Vilho?'

'*So far in the green. The engine is tilted forward at a sharp angle. We must have nosedived into the swamp. All the driver's controls, the radio, are knocked out. But the generator is still turning over, cooling fins topside must still be out of water, and I can supply train power from here. For a little while more ...'*

'What do you mean?'

'Air conditioning is out in here too. Temperature going up pretty fast.'

'Hold on. I'll get you out as fast as I can.'

'What are you doing?' Alzbeta called after Jan.

'The only thing possible. You're in charge until I get back. Any problems Hyzo will help you. When the tanks arrive direct them to the engine of train two and I'll meet them there.'

While Jan climbed into a coldsuit, Eino made a tight bundle of a second suit.

'You should let me go, Jan,' he said.

'No. Keep the power up. I have to see what can be done back there.'

He exited as fast as he could through the rear door of the engine-room and heard it slam shut behind him as Eino shut out the burning air. Without haste – but without any waste motion – Jan unshipped the cycle from its housing, strapped the coldsuit into place, then lowered it on to the Road. Only then did he realize the sickening nature of the surface.

It was a charnel-house behind the engine. The alien creatures had been crushed, smeared, destroyed. A few maimed survivors, still driven by some unknown urge, were struggling painfully towards the jungle. The thick blue flesh and blood of the others coated the road. It was bearable just behind the engine, but when he swung on to the cycle and started back past the row of stationary cars it quickly became worse. The wide wheels had worked appalling destruction. Where the cars had skidded great smears of crushed bodies coated the surface. Finally he had to steer to the inside of the curve of the Road, skirting the burned areas, to find enough surface to ride on. It was dangerous here, but there was no other way to get by the carnage. Very slowly he went past the train and back into the bend in the Road.

Something very large, clawed and deadly, lurched out of the jungle towards him.

Jan had only a glimpse as it reared up; he threw full power into the rheostats and the cycle screeched forward, pulling away from the creature, skidding wildly as it bumped over the corpses. Jan fought for control, skidding his boots through the slippery muck, risking a quick look back over his shoulder. He slowed. The beast was feasting on the crushed bodies and seemed to have forgotten him.

Train two was ahead; a frightening sight. The cars were jackknifed over the entire width of the Road and into the jungle on both sides. The engine was over the edge and nose down in the swamp.

The destruction on the Road was forgotten now as Jan threaded his way towards the engine. The cause of the tragedy was instantly apparent. A great tree had been burned, then dozed off the Road. It had stopped the engine from plunging headlong into the water. But in stopping it a thick, broken branch had punched through the armoured glass of the front port. It had been a quick death for the drivers.

It would not be easy to pull that dead weight from the muck of the swamp. That would come later. Vilho had to be taken to safety first. Jan stopped behind the engine, then climbed carefully up the cables with the coldsuit bundled under his arm. He could feel the burn of the metal even through his thick gloves and wondered if the engineer was still alive inside. It was time to find out. He flipped up the lid of the phone next to the rear entrance and shouted into it.

'Vilho, can you hear me? Vilho, come in.'

He had to do this twice before a weak voice rustled back. *'Hot . . . burning . . . can't breathe.'*

97

'It's going to get a lot hotter if you don't do as I say. I can't open this door so you must have sealed it from the inside. Vilho, you have to unlock it. It's out of the water. Let me know when that's done.'

There was slow scraping inside and an endless time seemed to pass before the trapped engineer spoke again.

'*It's open . . . Jan.*'

'Then you're almost out of this. Get as far from the door as you can. I'm going to come through fast and close it behind me. I have a coldsuit for you. Once you get into it you'll be okay. I'm going to count five, then I'm coming in.'

As he said *five* Jan kicked the door open and dropped through it, throwing the coldsuit before him. It was much harder to close the heavy metal door because of the angle, but he managed to brace his feet against the engine mount and heave with his shoulders. It thudded shut. Vilho was huddled against the far wall, unmoving. His eyes opened when Jan pulled at him and he made feeble movements to help as Jan slid the thick suit up over his legs. Arms in, helmet on, front sealed, full cooling strength on. As the cool air poured over him the engineer smiled up at Jan through the faceplate and raised a weak thumb.

'Thought I was cooked for sure. Thanks . . .'

'Thanks to you everyone on the train is still alive. Will the engine keep supplying them with current?'

'No problem there. I checked it out and set it on automatic before the heat got me. It's a rugged beast.'

'Then we may get out of this in one piece yet. The tanks are on their way now. Let's find the car with Lee Ciou in it and see what is happening. He's in radio contact with my engine.'

'That'll be number six in line.'

They walked back down the train, stepping over the rapidly decomposing corpses of the beasts that had caused the trouble. Although the cars were across the Road at all angles the couplings and connections still seemed sound; tribute to the long-dead engineers who had designed them. The people inside waved excitedly when they saw them and they smiled and waved back. The angry face of Chun Tae-keng appeared at one of the windows, mouth working with unheard curses. He shook his fist at them and grew even more infuriated when Jan waved back and smiled at him. Vilho switched on the outside phone when they reached the door and they buzzed and shouted into it for a number of minutes before someone inside went to fetch Lee Ciou.

'Jan here. Can you hear me, Lee?'

'Is that Vilho with you? Then the drivers . . .?'

'Dead. Probably instantly. How are the people in the train?'

'Better than we thought at first. A couple of broken bones the worst that happened. The damaged car has been evacu-ated and sealed off. Chun Taekeng has some strong com-plaints to make . . .'

'I can imagine. He waved to us on the way back here. What about the tanks?'

'Due any minute now, I think.'

Then we may still get out of this, get these people out of here alive, Jan thought to himself. Though it wouldn't be easy. Two dead. The drivers would have to be replaced. How could the front port be mended? There was so much to do. And fatigue was grabbing at him again, fighting to pull him down.

Chapter Nine

By the time the two tanks came rumbling up, Jan had his salvage plan made and the preparations begun. He waved them to a stop, leaned his almost discharged cycle against the scarred metal treads of the first one, then climbed slowly and wearily up into the cab. For the first time in hours he opened the helmet of his coldsuit and breathed deeply of the cool air.

'A real mess,' Lajos said, looking out at the crippled train.

'Cold water, a bucketful,' Jan said, and didn't speak again until he had drained over a litre of the life-saving fluid. 'It could have been a lot worse. Two dead, that's all. Now let's see that the living stay that way. Give me that pad and I'll show you what we're going to do.'

He quickly sketched out the foundered engine and the first cars of the train, then tapped the car with his stylo.

'We'll have to disconnect all the power here, and that's being taken care of right now. The engine of train three is nosed up to the last car of this train and I have been back there jury rigging connections. There's more than enough power for both trains. Right now Vilho is down there disconnecting the power and communication lines, but not uncoupling from the train yet. From the angle of the engine I think that the weight of the train is the only thing keeping it from nosediving into the swamp. Now I want you to get two 500-tonne breaking-strain cables from this tank to the engine, attach them, here and here. Then back up just enough to get them really taut and lock your treads. When that's done we can uncouple the train and the other tank can pull the cars far enough away to give us access. We then get two more cables on to the engine, both tanks tighten up and on the given signal we pull her out of there.'

Lajos shook his head with concern. 'I sincerely hope that you are right. But there is a lot of dead weight there. Can't the engine help? Get a little reverse drive on the wheels?'

'Negative. There is no way of controlling them from the engine-room. But Vilho can cut the brakes on and off when we ask him, he's jury rigged a control for that, and that's about all we can expect.'

'No point in waiting then,' Lajos said. 'We're ready whenever you are.'

'Some more water and we start.'

It was awkward, exhausting work, made even more so by the deadly heat. Cables were hard to attach with the thick gloves of the coldsuits. They worked without a break until, bit by bit, it was done. Once the cables were attached the train was disconnected; the cables to the tank creaked when they took up the strain. But they held. The other tank had already lashed on to the front axle of the car to pull it out of the way. Because of the angle the first car had to be dragged sideways until it was clear of the engine. Impossible, normally, yet it could be done now because of the alien corpses that had caused the accident in the first place. Groaning and swaying the car was pulled across the road until it was clear. As soon as there was room enough the tank instantly dropped the cable and ground over to its position on the very edge of the road.

'All cables attached.' The signal came at last. Jan was in the cab of the second tank, supervising the ponderous yet delicate operation.

'All right. I'm rolling back to get tension on my cables. There we are. One, are you still taut?'

'*I am now.*'

'Good. Start pulling on the signal of *go*. Am I in touch with Vilho on the brakes?'

'*I can hear you, Jan.*'

'Then keep your hand on the switch. We are going to get your weight on the cables. When the strain gauges read 300 I'll signal you *brakes* and that's when you take the brakes off. Understand?'

'*No problem. Just pull me out of here. I don't feel like a swim.*'

A swim. If a cable broke or they couldn't hold the engine's weight it would slide forward into the water. Vilho stood no chance of getting clear. It wasn't to be thought about. Jan wiped the sweat from his face with his forearm – how could it be hot in the air conditioned tank? – and gave the order.

'Here it comes, one. The signal is one, two, three – *go!*'

The engine and gear train growled as power surged to the tracks. They moved slowly backwards, clanking a single tread as the cable stretched under the load. Jan watched the strain gauge as the numbers flicked over. The instant it changed from 299 he shouted into the microphone.

'*Brakes!* This is it! Keep the pressure, keep it coming!'

The engine stirred, shifting sideways – then stopped. The strain went up and up, approaching the breaking point of the cables. There was a safety factor built in, more pull could be applied. Jan did not look at the readout as he applied a touch more power. The cables vibrated, shook with the stress – and the engine stirred. Rolling backward slowly.

'This is it! Keep it coming. Watch the front wheels when it comes over the top and hit your power down. There it comes . . . now!'

It was done. Jan permitted himself one deep breath before he faced the next problem. The drowned cab and the drivers there. More weary than he wanted to admit he pulled on his coldsuit.

There was a burial. Brief, but still a burial, with the few men in coldsuits the only witnesses. Then right back to work. The cab was drained and Jan examined the damage. Jury controls could be rigged and improved later. He supervised the job himself although he was swaying with exhaustion. A small replacement port was set into the centre of a heavy steel plate and the whole thing crudely but carefully welded over the smashed front port. The driver would not be able to see much – but at least he could see. The air-conditioning came back on and the compartment began to cool down and dry out. Replacement controls replaced the damaged ones and were wired into place. As this was being done the tanks had carefully straightened out the jackknifed train and all the couplings were examined carefully for damage. It seemed all right. It *had* to be all right.

Hours later the trains started forward again. At a much reduced speed until final repairs could be made – but they were moving. Jan was not aware of it. He had collapsed on the bunk in the engine-room, unconscious before his head touched the pillow.

It was dark when he awoke, hours later, and climbed wearily back into the driving compartment. Otakar was at the wheel, his face grey with fatigue.

'Otakar, go below and get some sleep,' Jan ordered.

'I'm fine . . .'

'He is not,' Alzbeta said, most emphatically. 'He made me rest, and the others, but has had none himself.'

'You hear the lady,' Jan said. 'Move.'

Otakar was too tired to argue. He nodded and did as he had been told. Jan slipped into the empty seat and checked the controls and automatic log.

'We're coming to the bad part now,' he said, soaked in gloom.

'Coming to it!' Alzbeta was shocked. 'What would you call that part we have just finished?'

'Normally it would have been one of the easy stretches. The normal life forms there are usually no trouble. It is the ones we are starting through now that are the worst. Residents of eternal summer. All the energy they need from that white hot sun up there, all the food they can consume from the other life forms around them. It's kill and be killed and it never stops.'

Alzbeta looked out at the jungle beyond the burned edges of the Road and shivered. 'I've never seen it like this,' she said in a hushed voice. 'It all looks so terrible from up here in the engine with the unknown always sweeping towards us. When you look out of a car window it's so different.'

Jan nodded. 'I'm sorry to say it but there's far worse out there that we can't see. Animal life forms never noticed or catalogued. One time I put out nets, just for a few hours when we were going through here, and I caught at least a thousand different kinds of insects. There must be thousands, perhaps hundreds of thousands more. The animals are harder to see – but they are there as well. They are voracious and will attack anything. That's why we never stop out here until we're out on the islands.'

'The insects – why did you want to catch them? Are they good for anything?'

He did not laugh, or even smile, at her simple question. How could she know any better, having been raised on this deadened world? 'The answer is yes and no. No, they are good for nothing in the way we usually think of things. We can't eat them, or use them in any other way. But, yes, the search for knowledge is an end in itself. We are here on this planet because of the pure search for knowledge and the discoveries made thereby. Though perhaps that is not the best example I could have used. Think of it this way . . .'

'Malfunction reports from train eight,' Hyzo called through from the communication board. 'I'm putting you through.'

'Report,' Jan said.

'We seem to have some air intakes that are clogging up.'

'You know the orders. Seal them and recycle the air.'

'We've done that on one car, but there are complaints that the air is hard to breathe.'

'There always are. These cars aren't airtight – enough oxygen is getting in. No matter how bad the air smells it's still all right. Do not, repeat do *not*, allow any windows to be opened.' Jan closed the connection and called out to Hyzo. 'Can you put me through to Lajos with the tanks?'

The connection was made quickly enough; Lajos sounded exhausted.

'Some of these trees have trunks ten metres thick, takes time to burn through.'

'Narrow the track then. We can't be more than five hours behind you.'

'The regulations say . . .'

'The hell with regulations. We're in a hurry. We'll be back soon enough and we can widen then.'

While he talked Jan reset the autopilot, adding ten kilometres per hour to their speed. Otakar looked at the speedometer, but said nothing.

'I know,' Jan said, 'we're going faster than we should. But we have people jammed in back there, crowded like they have never been before. It's going to start stinking like a zoo soon . . .'

The nose radar bleeped a warning as they rounded a turn. Jan flipped off the automatics. Something big was on the Road – but not big enough to slow the engine. The creature

105

reared up to do battle as they hurtled towards it and Alzbeta gasped. A quick vision of a dark green body, bottle green, too many legs, claws, long teeth – and then the engine hit it.

There was a thud as they struck, then a jarring as they crushed the body beneath the wheels, then nothing. Jan flipped the autopilot back on.

'We have at least eighteen more hours of this,' he said. 'We can't afford to stop. For any reason.'

Less than three hours had gone by before the alarm came in. It was train eight again, someone shouting so loud the words were unclear.

'Repeat,' Jan said, shouting himself above the other's hoarse voice. 'Repeat, slow down, we cannot understand you.'

'... bit them ... unconscious now, all swollen, we're stopping, get the doctor from number fourteen.'

'You will *not* stop. That is an order. Next stop in the islands.'

'*We must, the children ...*'

'I will personally put any driver off the train if he stops along this Road. What happened to the children?'

'*Some sort of bugs bit them, big, we killed them.*'

'How did they get into the car?'

'*The window ...*'

'I gave orders—' Jan clutched the wheel so tightly his knuckles turned white. He took a deep breath before he spoke again. 'Open circuit. All car commanders. Check at once for open windows. *All* of them must be closed. Train eight. There is anti-venom in every car. Administer it at once.'

'*We did, but it doesn't seem to be working with the children. We need the doctor.*'

'You're not getting him. We're not stopping. He can't do anything other than administer the anti-venom. Hook through to him now and describe the symptoms. He'll give you what advice he can. But we're not stopping.'

Jan turned off the radio. 'We can't stop,' he said to himself. 'Don't they understand? We just can't stop.'

After dark there was more life on the Road, creatures that stood dazzled by the lights until they vanished under the wide wheels, things that appeared suddenly out of the darkness and were crushed against the windscreen. The trains kept moving. It wasn't until dawn that they came to the mountains and the tunnel, diving into its dark mouth as into a refuge. The Road climbed as it penetrated the barrier and when they emerged they were on a high and barren plateau, a rocky plain made by levelling a mountain top. On both sides of the Road the tanks were pulled up, the exhausted drivers sleeping. Jan slowed the trains until the last one had emerged from the tunnel, then signalled the stop. When the brakes were set and the engines off the radio hummed to life.

'This is train eight. We would like the doctor now.' There was a cold bitterness in the voice. *'We have seven ill. And three children dead.'*

Jan looked out at the dawn so he would not have to see Alzbeta's face.

Chapter Ten

The two of them were eating together at the folding table in the rear of the engine. The Road was straight and flat and Otakar was alone at the wheel. When they talked quietly he could not hear them. Hyzo was below with Eino, the occasional cry and slap of cards indicated what they were doing. Jan had no appetite but he ate because he knew he had to. Alzbeta ate slowly, as though she wasn't aware of what she was doing.

'I had to,' Jan said, his voice almost a whisper. She did not answer. 'Don't you understand that? You haven't said a word to me since. Two days now.' She looked down at her plate. 'You'll answer me or you'll go back to your family car with the others.'

'I don't want to talk to you. You killed them.'

'I knew it was that. I did not – they killed themselves.'

'Just children.'

'Stupid children, now dead ones. Why weren't their parents watching them? Where was the supervision? The families here must breed for stupidity. Everyone knows what kind of animal life there is in that jungle. We never stop there. What could the doctor have done?'

'We don't know.'

'We *do* know. The children would have died in any case, and perhaps the doctor and others as well. Don't you understand I had no choice? I had to think of all the others.'

Alzbeta looked down at her clasped hands, her fingers wrung tightly together. 'It just seems so very wrong.'

'I know it does – and it was not easy to do. Do you think I

have slept since they died? It's on my conscience if that makes you feel any better. But how would I have felt if I had stopped and there were more casualties? The children would have died in any case before the doctor reached them. Stopping would only have made matters worse.'

'Perhaps you're right, I'm not sure any more.'

'And perhaps I was wrong. But right or wrong I had to do what I did. There was no choice.'

They let it rest there; there was no simple answer. The trek continued, along the chain of islands, along the planed mountain peaks. At times they could see the ocean on both sides and, from this high up, it almost looked attractive. The teeming life could not be seen, just the white tops and the marching rows of waves. Very soon a blue on the horizon grew to a long range of mountains. Before they arrived at the southern continent Jan ordered a full eight-hour stop. All running gear, tyres, brakes, wheels, were inspected and all the air filters cleaned again, though they did not need it. Another jungle was ahead and there would be no stopping. It was not as wide as the one north of the island chain, but was just as virulent.

This was the last barrier, the last trial. They went through it in three days, without stopping, and into the tunnel beyond. When the last train was well inside the tunnel they halted to rest, then drove on short hours later. This was the longest of the tunnels for it penetrated the entire range. When they emerged into sunlight again they were surrounded by desert, sand and rock glinting in the lights of their headlights. Jan checked the outside air temperature.

'Ninety-five degrees. We've done it. We're through. Hyzo, contact all drivers. We're going to stop for one hour. They can open the doors. Anyone who wants to go out can. Just warn them about touching metal, it might still be hot.'

It was holiday, release from captivity, excitement. All down the rows of the trains doors crashed open and the exodus began. The ladders rattled to the hard surface of the Road and people called to each other as they climbed down. It was hot and uncomfortable – but it was freedom after the cramped discomfort of the cars. They were all there, men, women and children, walking up and down in the light from the windows and the headlights of the trucks. Some of the children ran to the edge of the Road to dig in the sand and Jan had to issue orders to discipline them. Other than the lumpers there was little of danger in the barren desert, but he could risk no more accidents. He gave them an hour and by that time most of them, tired and sweat-drenched, were back in the air-conditioned cars. After a night's rest they pressed on.

The brief autumn of the Halvmörk year was almost over and the further south they went the shorter the days became. Soon the sun would not rise at all and the southern hemisphere winter would begin, four Earth years of twilight. The growing season.

As the desert swept past the windows of the cars the passengers forgot all their discomforts and even suggested longer driving days. They would be home soon and that would be the end of their troubles.

Jan, driving the lead engine, saw the posts first. The sun sat on the horizon and the shadows were long. For days now there had only been the unchanging sand and rock of the desert. The change was abrupt. A row of fence posts flashed by, marking the limits of a baked and cracked field. First one, then another came into view, the outlying farms. There was cheering down the lengths of all the trains.

'That's a relief,' Otakar said. 'Here at last. I was beginning to get tired.'

Jan was not cheering, or even smiling. 'You are going to

be a lot more tired before this is all over. We have to unload the corn and turn the trains around.'

'Don't remind me. You're going to hear a lot of grumbling.'

'Let them. If this planet is to have any future at all it will be because we have the corn here when the ships arrive.'

'If,' Alzbeta said.

'Yes, there's always the "if". But we have to act as though it will happen. Because it will be the end of everything if the ships don't come at all. But we can worry about that later. I don't mean to be the skeleton at the feast. Let's stop these trains on the Central Way, set the brakes and see if we can't have a party tonight. I think everyone is in the mood for one. We can begin unloading the corn after a good night's sleep.'

The party was very much in the order of things, there were no complaints about that. With the air temperature now down in the eighties it could be held outside, with elbow room and freedom for everyone. When the trains halted for the last time between the rows of barren foundations the doors burst open. Jan watched them swarming out into the twilight, then climbed slowly down the rungs from the driving compartment.

He still had work to do. The first chairs were being taken out and the trestle tables set up as he went to the rear of the main silo building. After four years of torrid summer the thick walls still radiated heat as he passed. Dust was banked high against the heavy metal door in the rear and he kicked it away with his boot. There were two sets of mechanical locks on the door, and an electronic one. He used his keys to open them, one by one, then pushed against the door. It opened easily and the cool air rushed out around him. Once inside he locked the door behind him and looked around at the familiar scene. This Water Central Control was identical

111

with the one he had shut down in Northtown before leaving on the trek. These two control rooms were the only buildings that were permanently air conditioned and climate controlled. They made human life on the planet possible.

Before starting the programme Jan sat in the seat before the console and activated the scanners one by one at the water station, over 1500 kilometres away in the mountains above the coast. The first was mounted in thick steel and concrete on top of the station, and when it turned it gave a panoramic view. Everything was as it should be, he knew that from the printout which would have informed him, long before this, if there had been any kind of trouble. But he always felt he could not be sure until he looked for himself. Irrational of course, but all good mechanics have a touch of irrationality. You have to like machines to work well with them.

Solid and powerful, a fortress of technology. A featureless blank exterior of weathered concrete, over three metres thick. Some flying lizardoids were on a ledge of the building; they flapped slowly away when the eye of the camera moved towards them. Far below was the sea where waves battered against the solid rock. As the point of view changed the bins came into view, half-filled with wealth extracted from the sea, a by-product of the desalination process. There was at least a ton of gold in one of them. Worth a fortune on Earth, but valuable on Halvmörk only for its untarnished qualities for plating on the engines and field machines. The last thing in the slow circuit was the deep canal, stretching down the mountain to the black mouth of the first tunnel, two kilometres below.

Internal cameras revealed the starkness and strength of this giant complex of machines, built for durability and work. So well had it been designed that Jan had gone there in person just once in all his years on the planet. Inspection and maintenance were continuous and automatic. It was an echoing cathedral of science, visited rarely, functioning continually. For four years it had idled, the fusion generator muttering just enough to provide standby electricity for maintenance. Now it would come to life again. The program of startup was long and complex, self-regulating at every step, designed by the builders now centuries dead. They had built well. Jan switched on the computer terminal, received recognition, and keyed in the order to initiate startup.

There would be nothing visible for some time since internal checks of all components were the first step in the series. When the machine was satisfied that all was in order it would slowly raise the output of the fusion generator. Then the force pumps, buried in the solid rock beneath sea level, would go into operation. Silent, with no moving parts, they would begin lifting the sea water up the large pipes to the station on the crest above. They used a variation of the same magnetic bottle that contained the fusion reaction, modified to seize the water and push it away. Higher and higher the water would be pumped until it spilled over into the flash distillation section. Here it was vaporized instantly, with most of the water vapour drawn off to the condenser. Gravity took over then.

Jan had seen enough people, talked to enough people, and he relished the privacy now. He sat and watched the screens and the readouts for hours, until the first splashes of water fell from the outlets, turning into a roaring river just seconds later. Down it rushed, carrying sand and airborne debris before it, until it vanished into the tunnel. It would be days before the first dirty trickle worked through the tunnels and canals to reach the city.

A separate stream of thick brine splashed down a channel cut away in the side of the mountain to fall back into the sea below. He would wait at least a week before starting up the extractors that took all the elements and chemicals from the sea water. In the beginning all that was needed was volume flow to fill and scour clean the channels. All was as it should be and he was tired. The party, he had forgotten about it. It should be well under way by now. Good, perhaps he could avoid it. He was tired and needed sleep. He took a repeater from the shelf, it would monitor the water machinery at all times, and hooked it to his belt.

Outside the night was warm, but a slight breeze kept it comfortable enough. From the sounds the party was well under way, with the food finished and the drink flowing freely. Let them enjoy it. Even without the rigours of the trek their lives were monotonous enough. When the farming began again there would be no more festivities for years.

'Jan, I was just coming to get you,' Otakar said, coming around the corner of the building. 'Meeting of the Family Heads and they want you.'

'Couldn't they wait until we have all had some sleep?'

'Apparently urgent. They pulled me away from a very cold pitcher of beer which I am going back to. They've put up the dome and are meeting there. See you in the morning.'

'Good night.'

Jan could not walk slowly enough, and the dome wasn't far away. Now that they had finished this first journey they would be back at their complaints and bickering again. He had to talk to them, like it or not. Let them get it out of their systems so that in the morning they could all get to work unloading the corn. A Proctor at the door, complete with side arm, knocked when he came up, then let him in.

They were all there, the Family Heads and the technical officers. Waiting in silence until he sat down. It was The Hradil who spoke. It would have to be her.

'There have been grave charges, Jan Kulozik.'

114

'Who's in trouble now? And couldn't it have waited for the morning?'

'No. This is an emergency. There must be justice. You are accused of assaulting Proctor Captain Hein Ritterspach and of causing the deaths of three children. These are grave charges. You will be held in confinement until your trial.'

He jumped to his feet, fatigue gone. 'You can't . . .'

Strong hands seized him, and pulled him about. Two Proctors held him and there was Hein grinning, gun pointed.

'No tricks, Kulozik, or I shoot. You're a dangerous criminal and you'll be locked up.'

'What are you fools trying to do? We have no time for this sort of petty nonsense. We have to turn the trains around and go back for the rest of the corn. After that we can play your games if you insist.'

'No,' The Hradil said, and smiled, a cold smile of victory, empty of any human warmth. 'We have also decided that we have enough corn. Another trip would be too dangerous.

'Things will go on here, as they always have. Without you to cause trouble.'

Chapter Eleven

The Hradil had planned it this way from the very beginning. The thought was bitter as bile and Jan could taste the hatred that welled up inside him when he thought about it. Planned and carried through by the brain behind those serpent eyes. Had she been a man he might have killed her, there before the others, even if they killed him in return.

Underneath him the stone floor was hot, still burning with the heat of summer. He had his shirt off and under his head as a pillow, yet he still dripped with sweat. It must be a hundred or over in the small storeroom. They must have prepared this even before holding the meeting to accuse him; he could see the marks where the stored parts had rested before being dragged away. There was no window. The light, high above, burned continually. The metal door locked from the outside. There was a gap between the door and the stone and a flow of cooler air came through it. He lay with his face pressed close to it and wondered how long he had been here and if they would ever bring him some water.

Someone had to care about him – but no one had appeared. It seemed incredible that he could be Trainmaster one day, in charge of all the people and all of the resources of the planet, and a forgotten prisoner the next.

The Hradil. They did what she wanted. Her co-operation to have him bring the trains south had been a temporary expediency. She knew he could do the job. She also knew that she had to bring him low and humble him when the trip was over. He stood for too much change and too much freedom of choice and she would not have that. Nor would the others. They would take no convincing to connive in his downfall.

No!

Too much had changed, too much was changing to let her win. If she had her way they would plant the seed corn they had brought, hold the rest of the corn to turn over to the ships when they arrived. With an abject knuckling of the forehead no doubt, a happy sinking back to the old ways, the ways they had always known.

No! Jan pulled himself slowly to his feet. That was not the way it was going to be at all. If the ships never came they would all be dead and nothing else would matter. But if they did come then they would not go back to the old ways. He kicked and kicked at the metal door until it rattled in its frame.

'Shut up in there,' a voice finally called out.

'No. I want some water. Open this at once.'

He kicked, again and again until his head began to swim with the strain, until there was finally a rattling of bolts. When the door opened Hein stood there with a drawn gun, the other Proctor at his side. He still wore the cast and he held that arm towards Jan, waving it before him.

'You did that and you thought you could get away with it. Well it's not going to happen that way. You've been condemned . . .'

'Without a trial?'

'You had a trial, it was all very fair. I was there.' He giggled. 'The evidence was conclusive. You have been condemned to die for your crimes. So why should we waste good water on you?'

'You cannot.' Jan swayed, dizzy, and leaned against the door frame.

'It's all over for you, Kulozik. Why don't you crawl, beg me to help you? I might consider that.'

He waggled the gun in Jan's face. Jan shuddered back, too weak to stand, sliding towards the floor ...

Seizing Hein's ankles and pulling them from under the big man, sending him crashing back against the other Proctor. Jan had learned about dirty infighting from his karate teacher who had made a hobby of it; these men knew nothing about the nastier kinds of personal combat. The gun was clumsy in Hein's left hand and Jan pushed it aside as he pulled the trigger. There was just the single shot and then Hein screamed as Jan's knee came up full into his groin. The other Proctor fared no better. The fist in his ribs drove the air from his lungs. His gun was still in its holster when he was battered into unconsciousness by the savage chops to his neck.

Hein was not unconscious, but glassy-eyed, rolling in agony, clutching himself, his mouth a round O of pain. Jan took his gun as well – then kicked him solidly in the side of the head.

'I want you both to be quiet for a while,' he said. He dragged the still forms into the storeroom and locked them in.

What next? He was free for the moment – but there was no place to flee to. And he wanted more than freedom. They needed that corn and the trains would have to make the return trip. But the Family Heads had decided against this. He could appear before them, but knew that would accomplish nothing. They had condemned him to death in absentia, they certainly would not listen to him now. If The Hradil were not there he might convince them – no, he knew that would make no difference. Killing her would accomplish nothing.

The only thing that would make any difference, save his

life and possibly the lives and futures of everyone on this planet, would be some major changes. But what changes – and how could they be brought about? He could think of no easy answers. First things first – a drink of water. There was a bucket in the corner filled with water where the Proctors had been cooling beer. Jan took out the few remaining bottles and raised the bucket to his lips, drinking and drinking until he could drink no more. He poured the rest over his head, gasping with pleasure at the cooling shock. Only then did he click open the ceramic stopper on a beer bottle and sip from it. The rudiments of a plan were beginning to form. Yet he could do nothing alone. But who would help him? Doing anything at all would necessitate going against the will of the Family Heads. Or had they over-reached themselves this time? If his trial and verdict had been reached in secret he might very well get some co-operation. He needed information before he could do anything else.

The guns that he had taken from the Proctors were pushed inside an empty seed sack, the butt of one of them close enough to reach in a hurry. There was only silence from the cell: it would be some time before there was trouble from that flank. Now – what was happening outside?

Jan eased the outside door open a crack and looked through. Nothing. An empty street, dusty and drab under the twilit sky. He opened the door wide and stepped through, then strode steadily towards the silent trains.

And stopped. Had there been a massacre? Bodies everywhere. Then he smiled at his black thoughts. They were sleeping, of course. Free of the trains, safely arrived, rest after the storm; they had all eaten and drunk themselves into near extinction. Then, instead of getting back into the jammed and noisome cars, they had sprawled and slept where they dropped. This was wonderful; it could not have been better if it had been planned. The Family Heads must be asleep as well and they were the only ones he had to worry about at the moment. Moving quickly, and quietly, he walked down the lengths of the trains until he came to the Ciou family. As always things were still neatly organized here, the sleeping mats laid out in neat rows, women and children together to one side. He went past them to the still forms of the men, stepping lightly, until he found Lee Ciou. His face was calm in sleep, the worried crease always present between his eyes now erased for the first time to Jan's knowledge. He knelt and shook Lee lightly by the shoulder. Dark eyes slowly opened and the crease between them reappeared instantly as soon as Jan put a silencing finger to his lips. Lee obeyed the pantomime signals to rise silently and follow. He followed Jan up the rung ladder of the nearest engine and watched as he closed the door.

'What is it? What do you want?'

'I have your tapes, Lee. Your illegal ones.'

'I should have destroyed them – I knew it!' The words were a cry of pain.

'Don't concern yourself with them. I came to you because you are the only person I know of on this planet with the guts to break the law. I need your help.'

'I don't want to get involved. I never should have . . .'

'Listen to me. You don't even know what I want yet. Do you know anything about my trial?'

'Trial . . .?'

'Or that I was condemned to death?'

'What are you talking about, Jan? Are you tired? All that has happened since we arrived is that we ate and drank too much and all fell asleep. It was wonderful.'

'Do you know about a meeting of the Family Heads?'

'I guess so. They're always meeting. I know they had the pressure dome erected before they would release the beer. I guess they were all in there. It was a better party without them. Could I have a drink of water?'

'There's a dispenser right inside that door.'

So the trial had been a secret! Jan smiled at the thought. This was the lever he needed. Their mistake. If they had killed him at once there might have been some grumbling, nothing more. Well it was too late for them to do that. Lee came back in looking slightly more awake.

'Here is a list of names,' Jan said, writing quickly on an order form. 'The men from my own engine crew, all good men. And Lajos, he learned to think for himself when he took over command of the tanks from Hein. That should be enough.' He handed the list to Lee. 'I don't want to take a chance of being seen. Would you take this list, find these men and tell them to meet me here? They are to come quietly and quickly on a matter of the utmost importance ...'

'What?'

'Trust me for a bit longer, Lee. Please. I'll tell you all together what has happened. And it is important. But it is urgent that they all get here as soon as possible.'

Lee took a deep breath as though to protest – then let it out slowly. 'Only for you, Jan. Only for you,' he said and turned and left.

They arrived, one by one, and Jan controlled his impatience and their curiosity until Lee was back and the door closed again.

'Is anyone stirring yet?' he asked.

'Not really,' Otakar said. 'Maybe a few stumbling about to take a leak, but they're going back to sleep. That was quite a boozeup. Now – what is this all about?'

'I'll tell you, but I want some facts straight first. Before this drive started I had some heated words with Hein Ritterspach. He claims I struck him at that time. He is lying. There was a witness to all that. Lajos Nagy.'

Lajos tried to move away from their eyes as they all turned towards him. There was no escape.

'Well, Lajos?' Jan asked.

'Yes . . . I was there. I didn't hear everything said . . .'

'I'm not asking that. Did I hit Hein, just tell us that.'

Lajos did not want to get involved – but he was. In the end he had to shake his head. 'No, you did not strike him. For a while I thought someone would be struck, you were both very angry. But you did not hit him.'

'Thank you. Now there is one more thing that is not quite that simple. Some children died, of insect bites, when we were passing through the jungle. You all know about it. I had a difficult decision to make. I did not stop the trains so the doctor could attend to them. Perhaps I was wrong. Stopping might have saved them. But I put the safety of all ahead of the few. It is on my conscience. If we had stopped the doctor might have been able to do something . . .'

'No!' Otakar said loudly, 'he could do nothing. I heard him. Old Becker had him in and was shouting at him. But he is a Rosbagh and they only get pig-headed when shouted at. He was shouting back saying that he could have done nothing to save the children, other than administer the antitoxin which already had been done. He blamed the people who permitted the windows to be open, even Becker himself.'

'Wish I could have listened to that?' Eino said.

'You and me both,' Hyzo agreed warmly.

'Thank you. I appreciate hearing that,' Jan said. 'For a number of reasons. You've now heard the details of the two charges against me. I think they are false accusations. But if the Family Heads want me to stand trial on them I will.'

'Why trial?' Otakar asked. 'An investigation perhaps, but

a trial only after the charges have been substantiated. That is the only fair thing.'

The others nodded agreement and Jan waited until the murmured comments had died away. 'I'm glad we agree about that,' he said. 'So now I can tell you what has happened. While you were all enjoying yourselves the Family Heads held a meeting in secret. They had me seized and imprisoned. Then had a trial on these charges – without *me* being there – and found me guilty. If I had not escaped I would be dead by now because that was their verdict.'

They heard his words in utter disbelief. Their shock was replaced with anger as the truth of the situation sank in.

'Don't take my word for this,' Jan said. 'It is too important. Hein and the other Proctor are locked in and they'll tell you . . .'

'I don't want to hear what Hein has to say,' Otakar shouted. 'He lies too much. I believe you, Jan, we all believe you.' The others nodded agreement. 'Just tell us what we have to do. People must be told. They can't get away with this.'

'They will,' Jan said. 'Unless we stop them. Just telling people won't be enough. Can you see any of the Taekeng standing up to the old man? No, I didn't think so. I am willing to go on trial, I *want* to do it. But by the Book of Law. In public with all evidence heard. I want this whole thing out in the open. But the Family Heads will try to stop that. We are going to have to force them to do it.'

'How?'

There was silence now for they were waiting, eager to help. But would they go far enough? Jan knew instinctively that if they thought about what they were going to do they would not do it. But if they acted in unison and in anger they might do it. And once done they would not be able to turn back. They were thinking revolutionary thoughts – now they must consider revolutionary deeds. He weighed his words.

'Without power nothing moves. Eino, what's the easiest way to take the engines out of service temporarily? Remove the computer programming units?'

'Too big a job,' the engineer said. Immersed in the technical problem, not considering the enormity of the crime they were discussing. 'I would say pull the multiple connector plug to the controls. In fact pull the plug at both ends and take the whole cable out. Done in a couple of seconds.'

'Fine. Then we'll do just that. Pull them from the tanks too. Bring them to number six tank, the big one. Then we'll wake everyone up and tell them what has happened. Make them have the trial right now. When it's over we put the cables back and go back to work. What do you say?'

He put no emphasis on the last question, though this was the most important decision of all. The point of no return, beyond which there was no turning back. If they realized they were taking all the power of decision, the real power of the world, into their own hands they might have second thoughts. A moment's wavering and he was lost.

They were technicians, mechanics – and never thought of it in that manner. They just wanted to right an obvious wrong.

There were shouts of agreement, then they were busy in assigning the various tasks, getting the operation into motion. Only Hyzo Santos did not join in the excitement but sat with wide intelligent eyes watching Jan all the while. Jan gave him no assignment, and soon he was alone with the silent communications officer. He spoke only when the others had left.

'Do you know what you are doing, Jan?'

'Yes. And you do too. I'm breaking all the rules and making new ones.'

'It is more than that. Once broken the rules will never

124

be the same again. The Family Heads will not want to do this . . .'

'They will be made to do it.'

'I know. And I can put a word to this even if you will not. It is revolution, isn't it?'

After a long moment's silence Jan spoke, looking at the other man's grim face. 'Yes, it is. Do you find the idea distasteful?'

Hyzo's face broke slowly into a wide grin. 'Distasteful? I think it's wonderful. It is just what should happen, what is written in *Class and Labour, the Eternal Struggle.*'

'I never heard of it.'

'I don't think many people had. I got it from one of the ship's crew. He said it was an invisible book, listed nowhere, but some reference copies did exist and duplicates had been made of them.'

'You're on dangerous ground . . .'

'I know. He said he would bring more – but I never saw him again.'

'Easy enough to guess what happened to him. Then you are in with me on this? It will be bigger than you can possibly imagine.'

Hyzo clasped Jan's hand in both of his own. 'All the way! Every step of the way.'

'Good. Then you can help me with one thing. I want you to come with me to the warehouse where Hein and the other Proctor are locked up. They were ready to carry out the death sentence so they both know about the secret trial. They are our witnesses to what happened.'

A few early risers were already stirring as they walked back to the warehouse. The street door was still ajar as Jan had left it.

But the storeroom door was open as well and the two Proctors were gone.

Chapter Twelve

Jan took a quick look around; the rest of the warehouse was as empty as the storeroom.

'Where are they?' Hyzo asked.

'It doesn't matter. This means trouble so we had better start it before they do. Get them off balance if we can. Come on.'

They ran now, ignoring the startled looks, pounding heavily through the dust to the row of silent tanks. They were undisturbed. Jan slowed to a panting walk.

'Still ahead of them,' he said. 'We'll go on as planned.'

They climbed into tank six and started the engines. This would be the only piece of moving apparatus not incapacitated. Jan trundled it slowly down the Central Way and drew it up before the pressure dome.

People were beginning to stir now, but the preparations to immobilize the tanks and engine still went ahead smoothly. At first the conspirators had moved guiltily, trying to avoid being noticed, until they had realized that no one paid them the slightest attention. They were just technicians going about their usual inexplicable tasks. Once they had realized this they carried the cables openly, calling out to one another with secret glee. It was all very exciting.

Not for Jan. He sat at the tank controls staring at the screens, watching the first of the men stroll up with a set of cables; his fist, unnoticed, pounded slowly on the panel beside him. Then another technician, then a third appeared. Hyzo sat in the open hatch above and passed down the cables to Jan as they arrived.

'That's the lot,' he said. 'What do you want us to do now?'

'You and the others can just stay in the crowd, I think that's best. I don't want a confrontation or charges of conspiracy at this early stage.'

'That's all right for them. But you want someone to stand up there with you.'

'You don't have to, Hyzo . . .'

'I know. I'm volunteering. What happens next?'

'Simple. We get the people together.'

As he said this he punched the siren button and held it down. The banshee wail screamed out, warbled up and down piercingly. It could not be ignored. People asleep were suddenly awake, those already at work stopped what they were doing and ran towards the sound. As the Central Way began to fill, Jan turned off the siren and unclipped the bullhorn from the bulkhead. Hyzo was waiting for him on top of the tank, leaning relaxedly against the fusion gun.

'There's your crowd,' he said. 'They're all yours.'

'Over here,' Jan said into the bullhorn microphone, his amplified words echoing back at him. 'Over here, everyone. This is an important announcement.' He saw Taekeng appear in the door of his car and shake his fist. 'Family Heads as well. Everyone. Over here.' Taekeng shook his fist again, then turned as a man hurried up and said something to him. He looked back and threw a single shocked glance at Jan, then followed the messenger towards the pressure dome.

'Over here, everyone, up close,' Jan said, then switched off the microphone. 'Not one Family Head here,' he said to Hyzo. 'They're planning something. What do we do?'

'Nothing. That is nothing to start any trouble. Start issuing orders for unloading the corn for the return trip.'

'But they've changed that plan. They won't let us go back.'

'All the better – they've told no one about this either. Let *them* start trouble – here in front of everyone.'

'You're right.' Jan turned the bullhorn back on and spoke into it. 'Sorry to disturb your rest, but the party is over and we have to get back to work. We must return to get the rest of the corn.'

There were groans from the audience at this and a few people in the back started to shuffle away. Over their heads Jan saw Hein come out of the pressure dome and begin to push forward through the crowd. He was shouting something, his face red with the effort. There was a new gun in his holster. He could not be ignored.

'What do you want, Hein?' Jan said.

'You ... come here ... dome. At once ... meeting.'

Most of his words were lost in the crowd noises. He pushed forward angrily, waving his gun now to reinforce his authority. Jan had a sudden idea; he bent and spoke to Hyzo.

'I want that pig up here, talking. Let everyone hear what he has to say. Get the others to help you.'

'It's dangerous ...'

Jan laughed. 'And this whole thing is madness. Get going.' Hyzo nodded and slipped away; Jan turned back to the bullhorn. 'That is the Proctor Captain there. Let him through, please, he has something to say.'

Hein was helped, perhaps more that he wished. He tried to stop below and shout up at Jan, but was jostled forward and before he realized it he was standing next to Jan, still holding his gun. He tried to speak quietly to Jan – who pushed the bullhorn before his lips.

'You are to come with me. Get that thing away!' He slapped at it but Jan kept it close so that their voices boomed out over the crowd.

128

'Why should I come with you?'

'You know why!' Hein was spluttering with rage. Jan smiled back warmly – and winked at the angry man.

'But I don't know,' he said innocently.

'You know. You have been tried and found guilty. Now come with me.' He brought up the gun; Jan tried to ignore the whiteness of the man's tight knuckles.

'What trial are you talking about?' He deliberately turned his back on Hein and spoke to the crowd. 'Does anyone here know anything about a trial?'

Some of them shook their heads *no*; all of them were listening attentively now. Jan swung about and pushed the bullhorn close to Hein's mouth. Watching the gun and ready to strike if the man attempted to pull the trigger. Hoping he would condemn himself and the Family Heads before he did. Hein began to shout – but another voice drowned his own.

'That will be enough, Hein. Put your gun away and get down from that machine.'

It was The Hradil, standing in the doorway of the dome and using the PA system. It had to be her, the only one of the Family Heads with the sense to see that Hein was giving their game away for them – and the only one with the intelligence to react so quickly.

Hein deflated like a burst balloon, the colour draining from his face. He fumbled the gun back into its holster and Jan let him leave, knowing there would be no more inadvertent help from this quarter. He would have to face The Hradil and that was never an easy thing.

'What trial was he talking about, Hradil? What did he mean I had been tried and found guilty?'

His amplified words reached out to her over the crowd which was silent and intent now. Her voice answered the same way.

'He meant nothing. He is sick, a fever from his arm. The doctor is on his way.'

'That is good. Poor man. Then there has been no trial – I am guilty of nothing?'

The silence lengthened and he could see, even at this distance, that she wanted his death as she had wanted nothing else in her entire life. He did not move but waited like stone for her answer. It came at last.

'No . . . no trial.' The words were wrung from her lips.

'That's very good. You are right, Hein is sick. Since there has been no trial and I am guilty of no crimes.' He had her now, she was committed in public. He must push the advantage. 'All right, everyone, you have heard The Hradil. Now let's get to work, the return trip starts as soon as possible.'

'NO!' Her amplified voice rang out over his. 'I warn you, Jan Kulozik, you have gone too far. You will be silent and obey. There will be no trip for the corn, that has been decided. You will . . .'

'I will *not*, old woman. For the good of us all it was decided that we must go for the corn. And we will.'

'I have ordered you.'

She was raging now, as angry as he was, their booming voices godlike over the gaping crowd. Any appeal to law or logic was gone, any attempt to involve the spectators useless. They could not be cajoled, not now, only told. Jan reached into the turret of the tank and pulled out a length of cable and shook it in her direction.

'I do not take your orders. All of the tanks and engines are inoperable – and will not run again until *I* permit it. We are going for the corn and you cannot stop us.'

'Seize him, he is mad, kill him. I order it!'

A few people swayed forward, reluctantly, then back as Jan reached into the hatch and fed power to the fusion gun controls. The pitted bell mouth of the gun tilted up – then burst into roaring life sending a column of flame high into the air; there were screams and shouts.

The heat of fusion spoke louder than Jan ever could. The Hradil, her fingers raised like claws, leaned forward – then turned about. Hein was in her way and she pushed him aside and vanished through the door of the dome. The firey roar died as Jan turned off the gun.

'You've won this one,' Hyzo said, but there was no victory in his voice. 'But you must watch that one every moment now. In the end it will have to be you or her.'

'I don't want to fight her, just change . . .'

'Change is defeat for her, you must never forget that. You cannot go back now, only ahead.'

Jan was suddenly weary, exhausted. 'Let's get the corn unloaded. Keep people working so they have no time to think.'

'Hyzo,' a voice called out. 'Hyzo, it's me.' A thin, teen-aged boy climbed half-way up the tread of the tank, calling out. 'Old Ledon wants to see you. Said to come at once, no waiting, very important he said.'

'My Family Head,' Hyzo said.

'It's beginning.' Jan thought of the possible consequences. 'See what he wants. But whatever he asks you to do come back here at once and let me know. He knows you're with me, it must have to do with that.'

Hyzo jumped down and followed the boy – but the engineer Eino took his place. 'I've come for the cables,' he said. 'We'll have to unhook the family cars first . . .'

'No,' Jan said, almost unthinkingly, reacting by reflex. The cables, the immobilized vehicles, they were his only weapon. He had the feeling that great forces were already at work against him and he could not surrender that weapon now. 'Wait a bit. Just pass the word to the others that we will

131

meet here in ... say three hours. To go over unloading plans.'

'If you say so.'

It was a long wait and Jan felt very much alone. Through the front port he could see the people moving about; ordinary enough. But not ordinary for him. He had shaken the Family Heads up, caught them off balance, won a victory. For the moment. But could he hold on to what he had gained? There was no use in speculating. He could only work to control his impatience; sit quiet and wait to find out what their next move was to be.

'It's not good,' Hyzo said, climbing down through the hatch.

'What do you mean?'

'Old Ledon has forbidden me to go with the trains on the second trip. Just like that.'

'He can't stop you.'

'That's right, *me*, but I'm just one person. I know why I'm in this and what it means. I didn't answer him, just walked out. But how many others are going to do that? Right now the Elders are calling in every one of the technicians and mechanics. They will be told what to do – and they will obey. Which leaves us with a two-man revolution and no place to go.'

'We're not dead yet. Stay here, sit on those cables, lock the hatch and don't open it until I get back. Without them we're lost.'

'And if anyone should try to get them? One of our own men?'

'Don't let them have the cables. Even if ...'

'If I have to fight? Kill them?'

'No, we're not going that far.'

'Why not?' Hyzo was deadly serious now. 'The ends justify the means.'

132

'No they don't. Just do your best — without hurting anyone.'

The hatch clanged shut behind Jan and he heard the dogs being driven home in the catch. He jumped down from the treads and walked steadily in the direction of the dome. The crowd had dispersed for the most part but there were still a number of people about. They looked at him with curiosity — but turned away when he caught their eyes. They were passive, trained to accept orders, they would be no problem. It was the Elders he would have to deal with.

There were no Proctors at the entrance which was a help; he wanted no trouble with them. Jan pushed the door open quietly and stood just inside it. They were there, all the Family Heads, too busy shouting at each other to notice him yet. He listened.

'Kill them all, that's the only answer!' Taekeng's voice was cracking; he must have screamed himself hoarse.

'You're a fool,' The Hradil said. 'We must have the trained men to run the machinery. We must order them to obey us and they will do it. That is enough for now. Later when he is dead they will be punished, one by one, we will not forget.'

'No one will be punished,' Jan said, striding forward, as calm as they were angry. 'You stupid people just will not realize the kind of trouble we are in. If the ships don't arrive we don't get replacement parts or fuel. Our tanks and engines will be knocked out one by one and then we will all be dead. *If* the ships come they will need all the corn we can possibly get together. They will need it for starving people — and we need it as the only weapon . . .'

The Hradil spat in his face, the spittle striking him on the cheek, running down across his mouth. He wiped it away with the back of his hand and fought to control his anger.

'You will do as we say,' she ordered him. 'There will be

133

no more talk from you about do this do that. We are the Family Heads and we will be obeyed. There will not be another trip. You will . . .'

'You stupid old woman, can you not understand me? Are you so ignorant that you do not know that nothing will move until I permit it? I have parts of all the machines and they will not run until the parts are replaced. I will destroy these parts now and we will all die the quicker. I will do this at once if you do not permit the return trip for the corn. You do this and I promise to ask no more of you. When we return you are in charge as always. You issue the orders and everyone obeys. Is that agreeable?'

'No! You cannot tell us what to do.' The Hradil would accept no compromises.

'I'm telling you nothing. I'm asking you first.'

'It is not too bad a plan,' Ivan Semenov said. 'We lose nothing if they go back for the corn. And we did promise . . .'

'Ask for a vote, Ivan,' Jan said. 'Or does this cow frighten you all?'

Then she was calm, just that suddenly. The unabated hatred was still there in her eyes, but not her voice. 'All right, we will argue no more. The trains will leave as soon as possible. I am sure you all agree.'

They were confused, not understanding her sudden change. But Jan knew. She was not ready for a showdown now. And she did not really care if the trains went or not. What she wanted was his death, preferably a long and painful one. From now on he walked with that danger and accepted it.

'I know you will all agree with Ivan and The Hradil,' Jan said. 'We leave as soon as the corn is emptied. We will need all the new drivers . . .'

'No,' The Hradil said. 'There will be only men. It is not

134

permitted for young girls to be alone with so many. None of the girls will be allowed to go. Alzbeta will not go.'

She threw this last out as a challenge and for a moment he almost accepted it. Then realized he could lose everything if he insisted. He matched her cold calmness with his own.

'All right then, just male drivers. Get out of here and issue the orders to co-operate with me. Make it clear to everyone what is happening. No more lies.'

'You should not say that . . .' Ivan complained.

'Why not? It's true, isn't it? Secret meetings, secret trials, secret execution plans, more lying so that fool Ritterspach takes the blame. I do not trust one of you out of my sight. Leave and go to your families and tell them what is to be done. Only when everyone is sure what is happening will the machines be made operable again . . .'

'Seize him now and kill him,' Taekeng screamed.

'You can – but someone else will destroy the cables.'

'It is Hyzo,' Ledon said. 'He defied me like this one.'

'We will issue the orders,' The Hradil said. 'Go at once and do it.'

Chapter Thirteen

The trains were ready to go, had been for almost two hours, standing quiet in the darkness. The drivers were in their seats waiting for orders. Food and supplies for the trip were in the house car, along with an unhappy doctor-in-training Savas Tsiturides. Doctor Rosbagh said that his assistant was not completely trained, not able to be on his own. Tsiturides had fervently agreed. He had come anyway. Jan could not risk his men on this trip without some kind of medical aid. The last details had been seen to, the off-duty drivers were already asleep, and he could not make excuses much longer.

'Back in five minutes,' he said, ignoring the questioning looks of his crew. He climbed down from tank six, he would lead the tanks himself on the return trip, and walked back along the trains. This was the spot – but no one was here. It had been a risk to send the first message, madness to follow it up with a second. But he had had to do it. The Central Way was silent, it was the middle of the sleep period.

'Jan. Are you there?'

He spun about and there she was, by the warehouse. He ran to her.

'I didn't know if you were coming.'

'I had the message, but I couldn't leave until now, when they were all asleep. She has them watching me.'

'Come with me.'

He had meant to build his argument logically and rationally, explaining how important it was she keep the bit of independence gained. To perfect her technical skills. It was a good argument. He wasn't going to mention how he loved

136

her and needed her. Yet at the sight of her he had forgotten it all and just blurted out the words. Alzbeta recoiled, shocked.

'I couldn't do that. There are only men.'

'We're not animals. You won't be hurt, touched. It is important for you, for both of us.'

'The Hradil would never permit it.'

'Of course. That is why you must leave without permission. Everything is changing and we must make it change faster. If the ships don't come all of us have only a few more years to live. When summer comes and we can't make the trip – we burn. I want those years with you, I can't bear losing one day of them.'

'Of course, I know.'

She was in his arms, and he was holding her tightly, hard to his body, and she was not resisting or pulling away. Over her shoulder he saw Ritterspach and two Proctors running towards them. All the men carried clubs.

A trap, that's why Alzbeta had been late. They had intercepted his message, planned to catch them together. The Hradil must have arranged it all, was gloating now at her success.

'No!' Jan shouted, pushing Alzbeta away from him, crouching in defence, hands extended. The clubs were to beat him with, not kill him, bring him back for her justice. *'No!'* shouted even louder still as he dived under the swing of the first Proctor's club.

The swing missed and he hit the Proctor hard, hearing the air rush from his chest, slapping his forearm hard against the man's throat as he whirled to face the others.

A club caught him on the side of his head, slammed down on to his shoulder. Jan shouted aloud with pain and grabbed the man, caught his neck in an armlock, pulled him about as a shield between himself and Ritterspach. Luckily the big

137

man was still coward enough to hesitate, to let the other two take the punishment. Now he could wait no longer. He swung wildly, afraid to close, striking the Proctor Jan held so that the man cried out, swung again.

'Don't, please stop,' Alzbeta cried, trying to separate the struggling men. The first Proctor shoved her aside rudely and circled to take Jan from the rear. Alzbeta, crying, came forward again, just in time to step in front of Ritterspach's wildly swinging club.

Jan could hear the sharp, mallet-like crack as it caught her full on the side of her head. She dropped without a sound.

He wanted to help her, but this must be finished first. In his anger he could not be stopped. Tightening his arm hard so that the man he held tore at the pain in his throat, then went limp. Jan seized his club and spun the man's body about, ignorant of the club that struck him once, twice. Throwing the limp attacker into the moving one, following up with his own club, battering until both were still, turning about and going for Ritterspach.

'Don't ...' Ritterspach said, striking out wildly in defence. Jan did not answer, his club speaking for him, thudding into the other's arm so the fingers went limp and the club fell. Hitting again, catching the back of the Proctor Captain's head when he turned to flee.

'What is it?' a voice shouted. One of the mechanics running down the train.

'They attacked me, hit her, get the doctor, Assistant Tsiturides. Quickly.'

Jan bent and picked up Alzbeta gently, bending his face to hers, afraid of what he would find. More afraid not to know. There was blood, dark on her pale skin. Her breath slow, but regular.

He carried her carefully to the nearest car and took her inside, putting her down gently on the filthy rug.

'Where are you?' a voice called out. 'What has happened?'

It was Tsiturides, bent over the men on the ground. He straightened up from Ritterspach, his face shocked. 'That other one is unconscious. This one – dead.'

'All right then, there's nothing you can do for him. Alzbeta is in here, struck by that pig. Take care of her.'

The doctor pushed by and Jan watched while he opened his bag at her side. There were more running footsteps. Jan closed the door and looked at it. Then took the keys from his belt and locked it.

'The fun's over,' he said, turning to the men as they came up. 'They jumped me and I took care of them. Now let us roll these trains before there are any more difficulties.'

It was a stupid impulsive thing to do. But it was done. He had tried to do it by law, by asking The Hradil, by suffering the indignities of her rejection. Now he would do it his own way. There would be no going back from this either.

Buffers clanked together, the cars moved slowly at first, then faster and faster. Jan turned and ran towards his tank, waiting impatiently until the train had rumbled by, then hurrying over almost under the wheels of the next engine.

'Let's go,' he said, closing the hatch behind him. 'Move out ahead of the trains.'

'And about time,' Otakar said, gunning the engine.

Jan did not relax until the Central Way changed into the rock surface of the Road, until the warehouses had grown small and vanished behind the last car of the last train. Then the fence posts were gone as well and the last of the farms and he still kept watching the monitor screen. They could not be followed – so what was he watching for? The one engine left behind was immobilized as a power station. Who was he running from?

139

Chapter Fourteen

Jan decided that they would have to travel for at least four hours before they could make a stop. But he could not force himself to wait that long. Even three hours was too much; he had to know how Alzbeta was. It hadn't seemed too hard a blow, but she had been unconscious when he left. She might still be unconscious – or dead. The thought was unbearable; he had to find out. At the end of the second hour of driving he admitted defeat.

'All units,' he ordered. 'A short rest stop. Change drivers if you want to. Begin your slowdown now.'

Even as he issued the command he pulled the tank out of line, spun it 180 degrees on its treads and went thundering back along the line of still moving trains. He found the car in which he had left Alzbeta and the doctor, reversed and swung alongside it, slowing when it slowed, jumping down the instant they had stopped. The right key was ready in his hand and he unlocked the door and threw it open to face an angry Doctor Tsiturides.

'This is an insult, locking me in the way you did . . .'

'How is she?'

'This car is dusty, uncleaned, with no proper facilities.'

'I said – *how is she*?'

The cold anger in his voice penetrated the doctor's complaints and he took a step backwards. 'She is doing well, as well as can be expected under the conditions. She is asleep now. Mild concussion, no more than that I am sure. It is safe to leave her alone and that is what I am doing.'

He picked up his bag and hurried away. Jan wanted to

look in, but was afraid to waken her. It was then that Alzbeta spoke.

'Jan? Are you there?'

'Yes, here I come.'

She was propped up on a nest of blankets the doctor had put together, a white bandage around her head. Enough light came through the uncurtained window to show her face almost as pale as the cloth.

'Jan, what happened? I remember we talked, then little else.'

'The Hradil set a trap for me – with you as bait. Ritterspach and some of his men. Capture me or kill me, I don't know. Whatever they had planned misfired when you got in the way. I'm afraid I . . . lost my temper.'

'Is that a bad thing to do?'

'Yes, for me it is. I didn't mean it to end that way – but Ritterspach is dead.'

She gasped at this, a stranger to violence of any kind, and he felt her hand withdraw from his.

'I'm sorry,' he said. 'Sorry that anyone had to die.'

'You didn't mean to do it.' She said it, but she did not sound convinced.

'No, I didn't mean to. But I would do it all over again if I had to. Exactly the same way. I'm not trying to excuse myself, just explain. He hit you and you dropped, dead for all I knew. They had the clubs, three against one, and I defended myself. It ended like that.'

'I do understand, but death by violence, it is . . . strange to me.'

'May it stay that way. I can't force you to understand, or feel the way I do. Do you want me to go?'

'No!' The word burst out of her. 'I said that I found it hard to understand. But that doesn't mean that I feel any different about you. I love you, Jan, and I will always love you.'

'I hope so. I have acted irrationally, perhaps stupidly. That I did it because I love you is little excuse.' Her hands were cold in his. 'I can understand if you blame me for what I did next. Putting you in this train and taking you away. We were talking about it when they attacked me. I never heard your answer.'

'Didn't you?' She smiled for the first time. 'There can be only one answer. I will obey The Hradil always. But now that she is no longer here to give orders it is not a matter of obeying or disobeying. I can love you as I have always wanted to, be with you always.'

'Jan,' the voice called from outside, then twice again before he heard it. He felt he was smiling like a fool and held her gently for a long moment, beyond words, then pulled away and stood up.

'I have to go. I can't tell you how I feel . . .'

'I know. I'm going to sleep now. I am much better.'

'Do you want some food, something to drink?'

'Nothing. Just you. Come back as soon as you can.'

The co-driver of the tank was leaning out of the hatch. 'Jan, got a message,' he said. 'Semenov wants to know why the stop and when we can go on?'

'Just the man I want to see. Tell him we move on as soon as I join him in his engine. Let's go.'

Ivan Semenov was still Trainmaster. With the families and all their problems left behind, Jan had relinquished the lead engine to him. Any problems that came up now would probably be with the Road and he could handle them better from the lead tank. Jan climbed the ladder to the driver's compartment and Ivan started the trains forward as soon as he had closed the door.

'What is the delay about?' Semenov asked. 'Every hour is important now, as you keep saying.'

'Come into the engine room and I'll tell you.' Jan was

silent until the engineer had left and the hatch was shut. 'I would like to get married.'

'I know, but that is between you and The Hradil. I can speak to her if you like, the law isn't that exact as to which families the girl cannot marry into. A decision could be made. But it is up to The Hradil . . .'

'You misunderstand. You are a Family Head which means you can perform marriages. I'm asking you to do just that. Alzbeta is here, aboard a train.'

'It cannot be!'

'It certainly is. So what are you going to do?'

'The Hradil would never permit it.'

'The Hradil is not here to stop it. So think for yourself, just once. Make your own mind up. Once it is done there can be no going back. And there is nothing that evil old woman can do to you.'

'It is not that. There is the law . . .'

Jan spat disgustedly on the floor then rubbed the spittle into the steel plating with the sole of his boot. 'That for your law. It is an invention, don't you know that? There are no such things as families and Family Heads on Earth, or taboos about marriage between chosen groups. Your so-called laws are works of fiction written by hireling anthro-pologists. Societies to order. They scratch around in the textbooks and put together bits and pieces of vanished so-cieties and brew up one that will keep a population docile and obliging and hard-working – and stupid.'

Semenov did not know whether to be shocked or angry; he shook his head unbelievingly. A physicist with the basic laws of energy threatened.

'Why do you say these things? You can't mean them, you've never said anything before.'

'Of course not. It would have been suicide. Ritterspach was a police spy – among his other endearing traits. He would have reported anything I said when the ships came and I would be dead as soon as they found out. But with the ships not coming it doesn't matter now. Everything's changed. I can tell you about dear old Earth . . .'

'I'll hear no more lies.'

'Truths, Semenov, for the first time in your life. Let me tell you about cultures. Mankind created them. They are an artifact, invented the same way the wheel was invented. Many different ones, all working one way or another if they were to survive. But that is all a matter of history now with just two classes left on Earth – the rulers and the ruled. And quick death for anyone who tries to change things. And this final and monolithic society has even been transported to the stars. To all the fat and wealthy worlds that mankind has discovered. But not to all of the planets – just the comfortable ones. When there is a need to occupy a really uncomfortable planet, like this one, then the tame professors are called in and given their assignment. Supply us with a stable and docile culture, because any problems would slow food production and plenty of nourishing and cheap food is needed. A nice ignorant culture, because farmers can still be stupid and get their work done. But technical skills will be needed as well, so allowance must be made for that. So a bit here, a bit there, choose and select and balance and stir them all together and you have Beta Aurigae–3. This planet. Patient factory farmers, slaving their lives away in dim stupidity – '

'Stop this, I won't hear any more of your lies.' Semenov was shocked, numbed.

'Why should I bother to lie now? If the ships don't come we're all dead in any case. But until they do I intend to live like a man again, not a silent slave like the rest of you. At least you have a good excuse, you're enslaved by stupidity, lack of knowledge. I have been enslaved by fear. My actions are being watched, I'm sure of that. As long as I stay in line, cause no trouble, I'll be all right. I've been all right for years. The watchers like me here. A planet for a prison – and at the same time they can get value out of me from my skills. But they don't *need* me. If I cause trouble I'm dead. Meanwhile all of the years and money invested in my education are not going to waste. They sent me here to use those talents. With the strict instructions that I could live here in peace through the days of my years and I would not be bothered. But if I spoke one word about what life is really like off this planet, why then I would be dead. So I'm dead, Semenov, do you realize that? If the ships don't come, I'm dead. If they come and are manned by the same people, why then you speak a word – and I am just as dead. So I deliver myself into your hands and do it for the oldest reason of all. Love. Marry us, Semenov, that's all you have to do.'

Semenov was wringing his hands together, not knowing what to think. 'These are most disturbing things you say, Jan. To myself, when I am alone, I have had certain questions, but there has never been anyone to ask. Though the history books are most explicit . . .'

'The history books are dull works of fiction.'

'Jan,' the voice broke in from the engine room speaker. 'Call for you.'

'Patch it through.' There was a burst of static then Lee Ciou's voice spoke.

'*Jan. A little bit of trouble. One of the tanks threw a tread. They pulled to the edge of the Road and are working on it now. You should be up to it in a few minutes.*'

'Thanks. I'll take care of it.'

Semenov sat in introverted silence when Jan went out, was unaware that he was gone. The engine slowed down when the two stopped tanks came into sight. Jan gauged the distance.

'Slow to ten Ks as you pass, I'll hop off.'

He opened the door to a blast of torrid air. Next time out it would probably have to be in a coldsuit. He swung down to the bottom rung and hung there, then dropped off in a run, waving back at the engine which picked up speed again. Lee Ciou and two mechanics had the broken tread spread out on the rock surface of the Road and were hammering the retaining pin from the damaged section.

'Cracked link,' Lee Ciou said. 'No way to repair it. Metal's crystallized, you can see here at the break.'

'Wonderful,' Jan said, scratching the brittle metal with his fingernail. 'Put on one of your spares.'

'Don't have any. Used them all up. But we can take one from the other tank – '

'No. We won't do that.' He looked up at the sky. It's beginning to happen, he thought. The ships don't come and things wear out and they can't be replaced. This is the way it is going to end. 'Leave the tank here and let's join the others.'

'But we just can't leave it.'

'Why not? If we cannibalize spares now what will we use when the next breakdown happens? We leave it and we move on. Lock it up and when the ships come we can put it right.'

It took only a few minutes to get out the few personal belongings and to close the hatch. In silence they boarded the other tank and put on speed to catch up with the trains that had gone by. It was then that Semenov called on the radio.

'*I have been thinking a lot since we talked.*'

'I hope you have, Ivan.'

'*I want to talk to – you know who – before I decide. You understand?*'

'I wouldn't have it any other way.'

146

'Then I want to talk to you – I have some questions. I don't say I agree with you, not about everything. But I think I will be willing to do what you ask.'

The tank driver jumped, his hands twitching on the speed controls, so that the tank lurched abruptly at Jan's loud cry of victory.

Chapter Fifteen

The engineers who had built the Road must have exacted great pleasure from conquering nature in the most dramatic manner possible. This great range of mountains, labelled simply Range 32–BL on the Road map, could have been penetrated in a number of ways. A simple long tunnel could have done it, slicing through to the lower coastal ranges where the Road would have been easy to construct. The designers had taken no such simple solution. Instead the Road rose up in long and easy loops almost to the summit of the range, in fact it did cross the levelled peaks of some of the lesser mountains. And here it stayed. Piercing peak after high peak with straight-bored tunnels. The rubble from the tunnels had been used as fill to bridge the valleys between, then compacted again to solid rock with molten lava. The energy used to do this had been prodigal but not wasteful. The Road was there, a monument to their skill and craft.

At the entrance to the tunnel that pierced the largest mountain, there was an immense levelled area. The builders had undoubtedly used this as a park for their great machines. Some idea of their size could be gained by the fact that all of the trains, every engine and car, could be pulled up here at the same time. It was a favourite stopping place for the families, where repairs or servicing of the trains could be made, offering a chance to socialize after endless days in the same cars. They stopped there now.

A big advantage was the height – and the fact that Flat Spot was on the shadow side of the mountain. This made the temperature, while still hot, bearable enough to go about without coldsuits. The men walked slowly, stretching and laughing, glad of the break from routine, though they did not know the reason. Meeting, 2130 hours, by the lead engine. It made a pleasant change.

Ivan Semenov waited until they were all assembled, then climbed up on the makeshift platform of lubrication drums supporting a thick sheet of plastic. He spoke into the microphone and his amplified voice rolled over them, calling to them for silence.

'I have come to consult with you,' he said, and there was a quickly hushed murmur from the men before him. Family Heads never consulted, they issued orders. 'That may sound unusual to you but we are now living in unusual times. The pattern to our life and existence has been broken and, perhaps, may never be mended. The ships did not come when they should – and they may never come. If that happens we are dead and no more need be said. Because they did not come we have brought the corn, all that we could, to Southland and are now returning to get as much more as we can. To accomplish this the rule of the Family Heads was defied by you men. Don't deny it – face the truth. You defied us and won. If you care to know I was the only one of the Heads who agreed with you. Perhaps because, like you, I work with machines and am different. I do not know. But I do know that change has begun and cannot be halted. Therefore I am going to tell you about another change. You have all heard the rumours, so I will now tell you the fact. This is not an all-male expedition. We have a woman with us.'

This time the buzz of voices drowned him out, and the men moved about trying to get a better view of the platform to see who was there. The silence returned, gradually, when Semenov raised his hands.

'She is Alzbeta Mahrova, whom you all know. She is here

149

by her own choice. Her other choice is that she wishes to marry Jan Kulozik, and he does choose to marry her as well.'

After this he had to shout to be heard, begging for silence, turning up the volume until his voice boomed and echoed from the rock wall behind him. When he could at last be heard he went on.

'Quiet, please, hear me out. I said I have come to consult you and I am. As a Family Head I have power vested in me to marry this couple. But the Head of Alzbeta's family has forbidden the union. I feel I know what I should do, but what do you men think the decision should be . . .'

There was never any doubt. The roar of approval shook the rock with greater sound than the amplifiers had used. If there were any dissenting voices they were drowned in the sound of the vast majority. When Jan and Alzbeta appeared from the train they shouted even louder, picking him up and carrying him laughing on their shoulders, yet still too bound by the laws they were breaking to touch her.

The ceremony was brief but affectionate, different from any other they had witnessed because of the all-male audience. The questions were asked and the answers given, their hands joined together, their lives joined as well when the rings were brought forward. A toast was drunk by all present and the deed was done. But it was a single toast since time was pressing. Their honeymoon would be on the rolling trains.

Through the mountain range and into the eternal blasting heat of the tropical sun. They made better time than they had on the outward trip for the Road was clear and they were lightly loaded. The tank crews stayed far ahead and the only difficulty was crossing the drowned section of Road. The empty cars had a tendency to float and had to be brought over one by one with an engine at each end. The only ones who did not mind the delay were Jan and Alzbeta who were forbidden to help in the operation and were ordered to remain inside their car. It was the only wedding present that the hard-working men could give them and was appreciated all the more.

Once the water was passed the Road was clear again — though never empty of danger. The never-setting sun now had a brassy colour to it and there was an ominous haze in the air.

'What is it?' Alzbeta asked. 'What is wrong?'

'I don't know. I've never seen anything like it,' Jan said.

They were driving again, driver and co-driver of one of the engines. This way they were together all the time, work periods and sleep periods. They did not mind, in fact they revelled in the pleasure of their companionship. To Alzbeta it was the final satisfaction of her existence as a woman. For Jan, the end of loneliness. But this was not a world to allow unlimited peace and happiness.

'Dust,' Jan said, squinting out at the sky. 'And I can think of only one place it could come from. I think, but I can't be sure.'

'Where?'

'Volcanic action. When volcanoes erupt they hurl dust high into the atmosphere where the winds bring it right around the planet. I only hope this eruption was nowhere near the Road.'

It was closer than they liked. Within twenty hours the tanks sent back word of an active volcano on the horizon. The jungle here was burnt and dead while the Road was thick with great chunks of scoria and heavy with dust. They were working to clear a way through. The trains soon caught up with them.

'It's . . . horrible,' Alzbeta said, looking out on the blackened landscape and the drifting clouds of smoke and dust.

'If this is the worst we hit we are all right,' Jan told her.

They crawled at minimum speed when they passed the volcano for the Road could not be kept completely clear and they crept through the constantly falling debris. The volcano was no more than ten kilometres from the Road, still active, wreathed in clouds of smoke and steam which were lit by red flashes and gouts of lava.

'In a way I'm a little surprised that we have not had this kind of trouble before,' Jan said. 'It must have taken an awful lot of artificial earthquakes to build the Road. That's a matter of record. And the energy it takes to start an eruption is only the tiniest part of the energy that is released. The builders knew their business and did not leave until the seismic processes were reduced. But there can be no guarantee that they are all ended. As we can see out there.' He looked out gloomily at the volcano, now dropping behind them.

'But it's over,' she said. 'We're through.'

Jan did not want to erase her happy smile by reminding her that there would have to be a return trip. Better the happiness of the hour.

Then they came to the scorched farmlands and the immense silos baking under the relentless sun. Loading the corn began, a slow process because of the limited number of coldsuits. Nevertheless the work was continuous, one man taking over when the other ended his shift. Putting a newly charged powerpack into the coldsuit, careful not to touch the burning metal of the external fittings. Out into the heat to swing the discharge hose over the opening in a car roof, to fill it to overflowing. The car was moved on, the hole sealed, another appeared below. The Road was knee-deep in corn for they made no attempt to be careful; speed was more important than neatness. More corn would be left to burn than they could carry away. When the last train was being filled Jan consulted with Semenov.

'I'm taking the tanks out now. But I'm worried about the section of Road that passes the volcano.'

'You'll clear it easily enough.'

'I'm not concerned about that. The volcanic activity seems to have died down. But we did have that big quake some days ago. If we could feel it here, how must it be that much closer? The Road itself may be damaged. I want a good lead time.'

Semenov nodded reluctant agreement. 'I just hope that you are wrong.'

'So do I. I'll report back as soon as I get there.'

They ran at top speed and made the journey without a stop. Jan was asleep when they came to the volcanic area and Otakar, who was co-driving the lead tank with him, came down to shake him awake.

'Big drifts across the road, but otherwise it doesn't look bad.'

'I'll come right up.'

They left the other tanks with dozer blades to clear the Road, then ground ahead over the mountainous drifts. The air was clear and the volcano itself soon came into sight. Silent at last, with just a plume of smoke drifting from its conical summit.

'That's a relief,' Otakar said.

'I couldn't agree more.'

They went on until the tank was stopped by an immense drift of dust and rock that completely blocked the Road. All they could do was back to one side and wait for the tanks with blades. They caught up quickly because all they were doing on the first pass was making a cut big enough to let them through. They would return and widen it for the trains.

The driver of the dozer tank waved as he tackled the mountainous mass, and was soon out of sight behind it. *'It's* getting shallow again,' he reported by radio. '*Not deep at all on this side . . .*' His voice ended in a gasp.

'What is it?' Jan asked. 'Come in. Can you hear me?'

'*Better see for yourself,*' the driver reported. '*But come through slowly.*'

Jan ground his tank forward through the gap, saw the tread marks of the other tank, saw that it had backed to one side so he could see the Road ahead.

It was clear now why the driver had gasped. There was no Road ahead. It ended at the brink of a fissure, a small valley that must have been a kilometre wide at least.

The ground had opened up and swallowed the Road, leaving an unspannable chasm in its place.

Chapter Sixteen

'It's gone – the Road's gone,' Otakar said, gasping out the words.

'Nonsense!' Jan was angry. He was not going to be stopped. 'This fissure can't go on forever. We'll follow it away from the volcano, away from the area of seismic activity.'

'I only hope that you're right.'

'Well we don't have much choice – do we?' There was no warmth at all in the smile that went with the words.

It was slow and dangerous work once they were away from the hard surface of the Road. The burnt jungle was a barrier of stumps, with ash and dust-filled pits between that could trap a tank. They were caught this way time and again, one tank after another. Each time it happened a weary driver would go out in a coldsuit to attach cables to drag the trapped vehicle clear. The dust and ash clung to their suits and was carried back into the tanks, until everything was coated and filthy. After relentless hours of labour the men were close to exhaustion. Jan realized this and called a halt.

'We'll take a break. Clean up a bit, get something to eat and drink.'

'I have a feeling I'll never be clean again,' Otakar said, grimacing as the grit in the food ground between his teeth. The radio light signalled for attention and Jan flicked it on.

'Semenov here. How is it coming?'

'Slowly. I'm taking a wide swing in the hope we will be able to bypass the fissure. I don't want to have to make a second cut. Is the loading done?'

'*Last train filled and sealed. I've pulled the trains two kilometres down the Road. The spilled corn is beginning to catch fire and I wanted us clear of any danger.*'

'Yes, keep them well away. The silos will go next – will probably explode from the internal pressure. I'll keep you informed of our progress.'

They went through two more sleep periods, locked in the filthy tanks, before they reached the volcanic fissure again. Jan saw it appear suddenly as the burnt tree he was pushing aside disappeared over the edge. He jammed on both brakes, then wiped the inside of the front port as the clouds of ash settled outside.

'It's still there,' Otakar said, unable to keep the despair from his voice.

'Yes – but it's no more than a hundred metres wide. If it's no deeper we'll just start filling it and we won't have to go any further.'

It was just possible. As the tanks widened and levelled the new track they had cut, the debris was pushed over the edge. Fusion guns burned and compacted it while more and more rubble was added to the growing mound. Eventually it reached the top and the first tank clanked gingerly forward on to the new surface. It held.

'I want more fill-in there,' Jan ordered. 'Keep the fusion guns on it too. Those engines and trains are a lot heavier than these tanks. We'll split into two groups. One to compact the fill, the other to cut a track back to the Road on the other side. I'll get the trains up behind us, ready to cross as soon as we're done.'

It was a rough and ready job, the best they could do. They laboured for more than a hundred hours before Jan was satisfied with the result.

'I'm going to bring the first train over. The rest of you stand by.'

He had not been out of his clothes since they had started the job; his skin was smeared and black, his eyes red-rimmed and sore. Alzbeta gasped when she saw him – when he looked in the mirror and saw why he had to smile himself.

'If you make some coffee I'll wash and change. That was not a job I would like to do again.'

'It's all finished then?'

'All except getting the trains over. I've emptied everyone out of the first one and as soon as I finish this I'll take it through.'

'Couldn't someone else drive it? Why does it have to be you?'

Jan drank his coffee in silence, then put down the empty cup and stood. 'You know why. Ride in the second train and I'll see you on the other side.'

There was fear in her tight-clamped arms, but she said nothing more as she kissed him, then watched him leave. She wanted to ride with him, but knew what his answer would be without asking. He would do this alone.

With the automatic guidance disconnected the train turned away from the centre of the Road towards the raw gash that had been slashed through the burnt jungle. The engine left the smooth Road surface and rose and fell as it ground along. Obediently, one by one, the cars tracked behind it, following in its deep-cut wheel tracks.

'So far no problems,' Jan said into the microphone. 'Bumpy but not bad at all. I'm holding at five Ks all the way. I want the other drivers to do the same.'

He didn't stop when he came to the filled-in fissure but ground steadily forward out on to its surface. Under the pressure of the engine's weight stones and gravel cracked free from the sides of the embankment and rattled into the depths. On both sides the tank drivers watched in tense silence. Jan looked down from the height of the engine and could see the far edge approaching slowly; on either side there was only emptiness. He kept his eyes fixed on the edge and the engine centred in the very middle of the dike.

'He's over!' Otakar shouted into his radio. 'All cars tracking well. No subsidence visible.'

Reaching the Road again was an easy task, once the tension of the crossing was behind. He pulled the train to the far side and ran forward until all of the cars were in the clear. Only then did he pull on his coldsuit and change over to the tank that had followed him.

'Let's get back to the gap,' he ordered then turned to the radio. 'We're going to bring the trains over one at a time, slowly. I want only one train at a time on the new sections so we can reach it easily in case of difficulties. All right – start the second one now.'

He was waiting at the edge of the chasm when the train appeared, clouds of dust and smoke billowing out from under its wheel. The driver kept his engine centred on the wheel marks of Jan's train on the embankment and crossed without difficulty and went on. The next train and the next crossed, and they came in a steady stream after that.

It was the thirteenth train that ran into trouble.

'Lucky thirteen,' Jan said to himself as it appeared on the far edge. He rubbed his sore eyes and yawned.

The engine came on and was half-way over when it started to tilt. Jan grabbed for the microphone but before he could say anything there was a subsidence and the engine tilted more and more in massive slow motion.

Then it was gone, suddenly. Over the edge and down, with the cars hurtling after it one after another in a string of death, crashing to the bottom in an immense bursting cloud of debris with car after car folded one after the other in a crushed mass of destruction.

No one came out of the wreck alive. Jan was one of the first who was lowered down at the end of a cable to search among the horribly twisted metal. Others joined him and they searched in silence under the unending glare of the sun. But found nothing. In the end they abandoned the search, leaving the dead men entombed in the ruins. The embankment was repaired, strengthened, compacted. The other trains crossed without trouble and, once they were assembled on the Road, the return trek began.

No one spoke the thought aloud, but they all felt it. It had to be worth it, the corn, bringing it from pole to pole of the planet. The men's deaths had to mean something. The ships had to come. They were late – but they *had* to come.

They were familiar with the Road now, weary of it. The water crossing was made, the kilometres rolled by steadily, the sun shone through unending heat and the trip went on. There were delays, breakdowns, and two cars were cannibalized for parts and left behind. And one more tank. The output of all the engines was dropping steadily so that they had to run at slower speed than usual.

It was not joy that possessed them when they came out of sunshine into the twilight, but rather the end of a great weariness and the desire to rest at last. They were no more than ten hours away from their destination when Jan called a halt.

'Food and drinks,' he said. 'We need some kind of celebration.'

They agreed on that, but it was a subdued party at best. Alzbeta sat next to Jan and, while no one there envied them, the men looked forward to the next day and wives of their own who were waiting. They had been in touch with Southtown by Radio so the seven dead men in their metal tomb were known to those who were waiting.

'This is a party, not a wake,' Otakar said. 'Drink up your beer and I'll pour you another.'

Jan drained his glass as instructed and held it out for a refill. 'I'm thinking about the arrival,' he said.

'We all are, but more so you and I,' Alzbeta said, moving closer at the thought of separation. 'She can't take you from me.'

She did not have to be named. The Hradil, absent so long, was close again, ready to affect their lives.

'We are all with you,' Otakar told them. 'We were all witnesses at your wedding and were part of it. The Family Heads may protest but there is nothing they can do. We've made them see reason before – we can do it again. Semenov will back us up.'

'This is my fight,' Jan said.

'Ours. It has been since we took over the engines and made them knuckle under for the second trip. We can do that again if we have to.'

'No, Otakar, I don't think so.' Jan looked down the smooth length of the Road that vanished at the horizon. 'We had something to fight for then. Something physical that affected all of us. The Hradil will try to cause trouble but Alzbeta and I will handle it.'

'And me,' Semenov said. 'I will have to explain my actions, account for them. It is against the law . . .'

'The law as written here,' Jan said. ' A little work of fiction to keep the natives subdued and quiet.'

'Will you tell them that, all the things you told me?'

'I certainly will. I'll tell the Heads and I'll tell everyone else. The truth has to come out sometime. They probably won't believe it, but they'll be told.'

After they slept they went on. Jan and Alzbeta had little rest, nor did they want it. They felt closer than they had ever been and their lovemaking had a frantic passion to it. Neither spoke of it, but they feared for the future.

They had good cause. There was no reception, no crowds to welcome them. The men understood that. They talked a bit, said good-bye to one another, then went to find their families. Jan and Alzbeta stayed on the train, watching the door. They did not have long to wait for the expected knock. There were four armed Proctors there.

'Jan Kulozik, you are under arrest . . .'

'Under whose authority? For what reason?'

'You have been accused of murdering Proctor Captain Ritterspach.'

'That can be explained, witnesses—'

'You will come with us to detention. Those are our orders. This woman is to be returned to her family at once.'

'*No!*'

It was Alzbeta's cry of terror that roused Jan. He tried to go to her, protect her, but was shot at once. A weak charge, minimum setting for the energy gun, enough to stop him but not kill him.

He lay on the floor, conscious but unable to move, able only to watch as they dragged her out.

Chapter Seventeen

It was obvious to Jan that his homecoming reception had been planned with infinite care and sadistic precision. The Hradil of course. Once before she had had him arrested, but the job had been bungled. Not this time. She had not revealed herself, but her careful touch was everywhere. No reception for their return, no crowds. No chance to unite his men and the others behind him. Divide and rule, most skilfully done. A murder charge, that was good, a man had been killed so the charge was certainly in order. And he had resisted arrest just to make her job easier, just as she had undoubtedly assumed he would. She had out-thought him and she had won. She was out there drawing the web tight around him, while he sat in the carefully prepared cell. No rude storeroom this time that might arouse sympathy, but proper quarters in one of the thick-walled permanent buildings. A barred, narrow slit of a window on the outside wall, sink and sanitary facilities, a comfortable bunk, reading matter, television – and a solid steel door with a lock on the other side. Jan lay on the bunk staring unseeingly at the ceiling, looking for a way out. He felt the eyes of the Proctor on him, staring in through the plastered observation window in the wall, and he rolled to face away.

There would be a trial. If it were at all fair his plea of self defence would have to be accepted. Five Family Heads would be the judges, that was the law, and all would have to agree on a sentence of guilty. Semenov, one of the oldest Heads would sit on the bench. There was a chance.

'You have a visitor,' the guard said, his voice rasping

from the speaker just below the window. He moved aside and Alzbeta stood in his place.

Happy as he was to see her it was torture to press his hands to the cold plasteel surface, to see her fingers a close centimetre beyond his, yet to be unable to touch them.

'I asked to see you,' she said. 'I thought they would say no, but there was no trouble.'

'Of course. No lynch parties this time. She learns by her mistakes. This time by the book, by the rule of law and order. Visitors allowed, why of course. Final verdict, guilty of course.'

'There has to be a chance. You will fight?'

'Don't I always?' He forced himself to smile, for her sake, and was answered by the slightest smile in return. 'There is really no case. You witnessed the attack, were struck yourself, the other Proctors will have to agree with that under oath. They had all the clubs, I fought back when you were struck down. Ritterspach's death was accidental – they'll have to admit that. I'll defend myself, but there is one thing you can do to help me.'

'Anything!'

'Get me a copy of the legal tapes that I can play on the TV here. I want to bone up on the niceties of the Book of Law. Build a strong case.'

'I'll bring them as soon as I can. They said I could bring you food, I'll cook something special. And another thing,' she looked sideways out of the corners of her eyes, then lowered her voice. 'You have friends. They want to help you. If you were out of here . . .'

'*No!* Tell them no as emphatically as you can. I don't want to escape. I'm enjoying the rest. Not only is there no place to hide on this planet but I want to do this the right way. Defeat that woman by law. It is the only way.'

He did not tell Alzbeta that undoubtedly every word they

163

spoke through the communicator was being recorded. He did not want anyone getting into trouble on his account. And basically what he said was true. This had to be done the legal way now. If he had to communicate there were ways. The cell was clear, there were no visual bugs. She could read a note if he held it up to the observation window. He would save that for any emergencies.

They talked more but there was little to say. The ache of being close to her without touching her was becoming unbearable and he was relieved when the guard told her it was time to go.

His second visitor was Hyzo Santos. The communications officer was undoubtedly well aware that their talk would be listened to and kept their conversation on neutral grounds.

'Alzbeta tells me you are enjoying your rest, Jan.'

'I have little choice, do I?'

'Make the most of the quiet, you'll be back in action soon enough. I brought that copy of the Book of the Law that you asked about. I guess the guard will give it to you.'

'My thanks. I'll want to study it closely.'

'Very closely, if I were you.' Hyzo's scowl deepened. 'There have been some meetings of Family Heads. Only rumours of course, but there was an announcement this morning and the rumours are true. Ivan Semenov is no longer Head of his family.

'They can't do that!'

'They can, and they did. You'll find the process described in your copy of the Book of the Law. He broke the law when he officiated at Alzbeta's marriage without The Hradil's permission. Poor Semenov is stripped of all rank and title. He's working as a cook's helper.'

'The marriage is still valid, isn't it?' Jan asked worriedly.

'Absolutely. Nothing can touch that. A marriage bond is

a marriage bond and completely unbreakable as you know. But, the judges have been chosen for the trial . . .'

Sudden realization shook Jan. 'Of course. He's no longer a Family Head so Semenov won't be there. It will be The Hradil and four more of her kind.'

'I'm afraid so. But justice will be seen to be done. No matter how prejudiced they are they can't go against the law in open court. You have a lot of people on your side.'

'And a lot more who are looking forward to me getting it in the neck, too.'

'You've said it yourself. You can't change people overnight. Even though there are changes going on the people don't like it. This is a conservative world and people, for the most part, are troubled by change. That's on your side now. The trial will be a legal one and you will have to get off.'

'I wish I shared your enthusiasm.'

'You will as soon as you have eaten some of the chicken and dumpling stew Alzbeta sent with the tape. That is if the jailers leave you any of it after it is searched for weapons.'

All according to law. No doubts about it. Then why was he so worried? There were less than seven days left to the trial and Jan busied himself with a study of the Book of the Law which, admittedly he had never looked at very closely before. It proved to be a simplified version of Earth Commonwealth law. A great deal had been pruned away – there was certainly no need to go into the details of illegal counterfeiting on a world without money. Or space barratry. But ironclad additions had been written into it that gave the Family Heads the power of absolute rule. What little bits of personal freedom had been in the original were totally missing here.

On the day of the trial Jan shaved carefully, then pulled on the clean clothes that had been brought for him. He carefully pinned on his badge of rank. He was Maintenance

Captain and he wanted everyone to remember it. When the guards came he was ready to go, almost eager. But he drew back when they produced the wristcuffs.

'No need for those,' he said. 'I'm not going to attempt to escape.'

'Orders,' the Proctor said, Scheer, the same one Jan had felled with the club. He stood out of range with his gun raised. There was no point in resisting. Jan shrugged and held out his arms.

It was more like a feast day than a trial – and it looked like the entire population had decided to do just that. There was little work to be done since the seed corn had not been planted. So they came, all of them, filling the Central Way from side to side. Family groups, with food and drink, prepared for a long siege. But there were no children there, under the age of sixteen they were forbidden to attend trials because of the banned things that might be said. So the older children were watching the younger ones and hating it.

No building could have held this crowd so the trial would take place outdoors, under the changeless twilight sky. A platform had been erected with seats for judges and defendant. A speaker system had been hooked up so that everyone could hear. There was a carnival feelings in the air, some free entertainment so they could all forget their troubles. And the ships that never came.

Jan climbed the flight of steps and sat down in the box. Then examined the judges. The Hradil, of course. Her presence there had been as assured as the law of gravity. And Chun Taekeng, Senior Elder, his place guaranteed as well. An unexpected face, old Krelshev. Of course – he would have taken over as Elder when Semenov was unseated. A man of no intelligence and less nerve. A tool like the other two sitting next to him. The Hradil was the only one that counted today. She was leaning towards them, instructing them no doubt, then straightened up and turned to face Jan. The wrinkled face cold as ever, the eyes unemotional icy pits. But she smiled when she looked at him, ever so slightly, but undoubtedly a smile there though it vanished in an instant. A victory smile; she was so sure of herself. Jan forced himself not to react, to sit in stony and expressionless silence. Any emotion he displayed during this trial could only do him harm. But he still wondered what she was smiling at. It was not long before he found out.

'Silence, silence in court,' The Hradil called out and her amplified voice spread down the Central Way, bouncing from the buildings on each side. She said it just once and the response was instant. This was a most serious moment.

'We are here today to judge one of our number,' she said. 'Jan Kulozik the Maintenance Captain. Grave charges have been levelled and this court has been assembled. I ask the technician, is the recorder operating?'

'It is.'

'Then proper records will be kept. Let the record show that Kulozik was accused by Proctor Scheer of murdering Proctor Captain Ritterspach. This is a grave charge and the Elders in conference investigated the matter. It was discovered that witnesses to the so-called murder differed with Proctor Scheer. It appears that Ritterspach died when Kulozik was defending himself from an unprovoked attack. Self defence is not a crime. Therefore it was deduced that the death was accidental and charges of murder have been dropped. Proctor Scheer has been admonished for his enthusiasm.'

What did it mean? The crowd was just as much at a loss as Jan was and a murmur swept through the watchers, silenced when The Hradil lifted her hand. Jan did not like it. All he knew was that with the charges dismissed he was still cuffed. And that oaf Scheer had the nerve to be grinning at him. Admonished and now smiling? More was going on here than was apparent and Jan was determined to strike first. He stood and leaned close to the microphone.

'I am pleased that the truth has come out. Therefore please free my wrists – '

'Prisoner will be seated,' The Hradil said. The two Proctors slammed Jan back into the chair. It was not over yet.

'Far graver charges have been levelled against the prisoner. He is charged with inciting to riot, with disloyalty, with disloyal actions, with disloyal propaganda, and with the most serious crime of all. Treason.

'All of these crimes are most grave, the final one the most grave of all. It carries with it the death penalty. Jan Kulozik is guilty of all of these crimes and will be proven so today. His execution will take place within a day of the trial, for that is the law.'

Chapter Eighteen

There was shouting from the immense crowd, questions. Angry men pushed forward, Jan's friends, but stopped when all twelve of the Proctors drew up in a line in front of the platform, weapons ready.

'Keep your distance,' Proctor Scheer called out. 'Everyone stay back. These guns are set on maximum discharge.'

The men called out but did not draw too close to the ready weapons. The Hradil's amplified voice washed over them.

'There will be no disturbances. Proctor Captain Scheer has orders to shoot if he must. There may be dissident elements in the crowd who will attempt to help the prisoner. They must not be allowed to.'

Jan sat still in the box, realizing now what was happening. Admonished one minute, Proctor Captain the next; Scheer was doing all right. The Hradil had him firmly in her hand. Had Jan as well. He had relaxed his defences, thought about the crime of murder, never realizing that this charge was just a front for the real charges. There was no way out now; the trial would have to continue. As soon as The Hradil stopped talking he spoke loudly into the microphone.

'I demand that this farce be ended and that I be freed. If there is any treason here it is on the part of that old woman who wants to see us all dead...'

He stopped talking when his microphone was cut off. There was no escaping the situation, he only hoped that he could make The Hradil lose her temper. She was possessed with anger, he could tell that by the hiss in her voice when she spoke, but she still kept it under control.

'Yes, we will do as the prisoner suggests. I have consulted with my fellow judges and they agree with me. We will drop all the charges, all except the important one. Treason. We have had enough of this man and his flouting of legitimate authority. We have been lenient because these are dangerous times and some leniency must be allowed, to get things done. Perhaps we were in error by allowing the prisoner too much freedom to act against the established ways. This error must be erased. I ask the technical recorder to read from the Book of the Law. The third entry labelled "treason" under the laws of rule.'

The technician ran his fingers over the keys of his computer, finding the proper section and displaying it on the screen before him. As soon as he had the entry correct he pressed the audio output. In commanding tones the law boomed forth.

'Treason. Whomsoever shall reveal the secrets of the state to others shall be guilty of treason. Whomsoever shall reveal the details of the operations of the authorities shall be guilty of treason. Whomsoever shall flaunt the majesty of the authorities and induce others to go against the authority of the state shall be guilty of treason. The penalty for treason is death and the penalty shall be exacted twenty-four hours after sentencing.'

There was shocked silence as the voice faded away. Then The Hradil spoke.

'You have heard the nature of the crime and its punishment. You will now hear the evidence. I will supply the evidence myself. Before the families and before the Heads of Families the prisoner mocked the authority of the Heads of Families, the duly constituted authorities here. When he was ordered to cease in his disloyalty and obey orders he defied them. He ordered that the machines be stopped by some mechanical means known to him, unless a second trip was made to get corn. This trip was made and many died because of him. By acting in this manner and causing others to defy authority in this manner he became guilty of treason. This is the evidence, the judges will now decide.'

'I demand to be heard,' Jan shouted. 'How can you try me without my being permitted to speak?'

Although the microphone before him was disconnected, those closest to the platform could hear what he said. There were shouts from his friends, from others, that he be allowed to speak. Not surprisingly there were other cries that he be silenced. The Hradil listened to this in silence, then conferred with the other judges. It was Chun Taekeng, as Senior Elder, who made the announcement.

'We are merciful and things must be done by the rule of law. The prisoner will be permitted to speak before judgment is passed on him. But I warn him that if he speaks treason again he will be silenced at once.'

Jan looked over at the judges, then rose and turned to the massed crowd. What could he say that would not be called treasonous? If he said one word about the other planets or of Earth he would be cut off. He had to play this by their rules now. There seemed little hope – but he had to try.

'People of Halvmörk. I am being tried today because I did everything in my power to save your lives and save the corn which is sure to be badly needed by the ships when they come. That is all I have done. Some have opposed me and they were in error and it will be proved that they were in error. My only crime, and it is not a crime, was to point out the new and dangerous situation and outline ways to handle it. Things we did have never been done before – but that doesn't mean that they were wrong. Just new. The old rules did not apply to the new situations. I had to act as strongly as possible or the new things would not have been done. What I did was not treason, but just common sense. I cannot be condemned for that . . .'

'That is enough,' The Hradil said, breaking in. His microphone went dead. 'The prisoner's arguments will be considered. The judges will now confer.'

She was arrogant in her power. There was no conferring. She simply wrote on a piece of paper and passed it to the next judge. He wrote and passed it along. They all wrote quickly; it was obvious what the word was. The paper was passed in the end to Chun Taekeng who barely glanced at it before he spoke.

'Guilty. The prisoner is found guilty. He will die by garrotting in twenty-four hours. Garrotting is the punishment for treason.'

There had never been an execution on this planet before, not in the lifetime of any of those present. They had never even heard of the means of punishment. They shouted to each other, calling out questions to the judges. Hyzo Santos pushed through the crowd, to the edge, and his voice could be heard over the others'.

'That's not treason what Jan did. He's the only sane man here. If what he did was treason then the rest of us are guilty of treason as well—'

Proctor Captain Scheer raised his gun, at point blank range, and fired. The flame wrapped Hyzo's body, charring him in an instant, turning the shocked horror on his face to a black mask. He was dead before he fell.

There were screams as those nearby pushed back, moans of pain from those burnt by the edges of the blast. The Hradil spoke.

'A man has been executed. He shouted aloud that he was guilty of treason. Are there any more who wish to cry out

172

they are guilty of treason? Come forward, speak plainly, you will be heard.'

She purred the words, hoping for a response. Those closest pushed back, on the verge of panic. None came forward. Jan looked at the body of his friend and felt a strange numbness. Dead. Killed because of him. Perhaps the charges were right and he did bring chaos and death. He stirred when Scheer stepped behind him and grabbed him by the arms so he could not move. Jan understood why when he saw The Hradil coming slowly towards him.

'Do you see where your folly has led you, Kulozik?' she said. 'I warned you not to defy me, but you would not listen. You had to preach treason. Men have died because of you, the last but moments ago. But that is at an end now because you are at an end. We will soon be finished with you … Alzbeta will be finished with you …'

'Don't soil her name by speaking it with your putrid lips!'

Jan had not meant to speak, but she goaded him to it.

'Alzbeta will no longer be married to you when you are dead, will she? That is the only way to terminate a marriage and this one will be terminated. And your child will be raised by another man, will call another man father.'

'What are you talking about, hag?'

'Oh, didn't she tell you? Perhaps she forgot. Perhaps she thought you might find the idea of her married to another repugnant. She will have a child, your child – '

She stopped, gaping, when Jan burst into loud laughter, shaking in Scheer's hard grip.

'Do not laugh, it is true,' she cried.

'Take me from her, take me to my cell,' Jan called out turning away, still laughing. Her news had had the opposite effect from the one she had wished for. This was such good news. He said that to Alzbeta when she came to see him in his cell after he had been locked away.

173

'You should have told me,' he said. 'You must have known better than that scruffy old bitch how I would react.'

'I wasn't sure. It was such wonderful news, just a short while ago. The doctor must have told her, I didn't know she knew. I just didn't want to bother you.'

'Bother? A little good news goes a long way in these bitter times. The baby itself is what counts. I could be killed at any time – but you will still have our child. To me that is the important thing. You should have seen that monster's face when I started to laugh. It wasn't until later that I realized it was the best thing I could have done. She is so evil she can't appreciate that others can have any wholesome or decent thoughts.'

Alzbeta nodded. 'I used to be hurt when you talked like that about her, it bothered me so. After all she is The Hradil. But you are right. She is all those things and more . . .'

'Don't talk like that, not here.'

'Because of the recordings being made? I know about that now, one of your friends told me. But I want her to hear, I want to tell her these things myself. She worked so hard to keep us apart.'

And in the end she is going to succeed, Jan thought, blackly. She has won. The sight of Alzbeta so near yet so untouchable was too much at the moment.

'Go now, please,' he told her. 'But come back later, do you promise?'

'Of course.'

He fell on to the bed, his back to the window, not wishing to see her leave. Then it was all over. Hyzo was the only one who might have done something to help him. But Hyzo was dead, angered by her as she must have planned. Killed by her as she had carefully planned as well. No one else could organize any help in the short time left. He had friends, many of them, but they were helpless. And enemies as well, everyone who hated change and blamed him for everything. Probably the majority of people on this world. Well he had done what he could for them. Not very much. Though if the ships came now they would have the corn waiting. Not that the people here would avail themselves of the advantage. They would bow like the peasants they were and go back to the fields and servitude, and slave their lives away for no reward, no future. Nothing. He had had the brief time with Alzbeta; that was worth a lot to him. Better to have had something than nothing. And she would have their son, hopefully a son. Or better a daughter. A son of his might have too much of his father's characteristics. A daughter would be better. The meek did not inherit the earth here, but perhaps they lived a bit longer with a little more happiness. All of which would be academic if the ships never came. They might be able to get most of the people through to the north just one more time with the decaying equipment. Probably not even that if he were not there to put things back together.

And he was not going to be there, because in a few short hours he would be dead. He hung heavily from the bars of the tiny window and looked out at the perpetual grey of the sky. The garrotte. No one here had ever heard of it. Revived by the rulers of Earth for the worst offenders. He had been forced to witness an execution of this kind once. The prisoner seated on the specially built chair with the high back. The hole behind his neck. The loop of thick cord passed around his neck with the ends through the hole. The handle attached to the cord that turned and tightened and shortened it until the prisoner was throttled, painfully, and dead. There had to be a sadist to tighten the cord. No shortage of them. Surely Scheer would volunteer for the job.

'Someone to see you,' the guard called in.

'No visitors. I want to see no one else other than Alzbeta.

Respect a man's last wishes. And get me some food and beer. Plenty of beer.'

He drank, but he had no appetite for the food. Alzbeta came once again and they talked quietly, closely, as close as they could get. She was there when the Proctors came for him and they ordered her away.

'No surprise to see you, Scheer,' Jan said. 'Are they going to be nice and let you turn the handle on the machine?'

Jan could tell by the man's sudden pallor and silence that his guess had been right. 'But maybe I'll kill you first,' he said and raised his fist.

Scheer lurched back, scrambling for his gun, a coward. Jan did not smile at the spectacle. He was tired of them, tired of them all, tired of this stupid peasant world, almost ready to welcome oblivion.

Chapter Nineteen

It was the same platform that had been used for the trial, the same public address system still set up. Nothing was wasted; everything carefully planned. But the chairs and tables placed there for the trial had been removed and a single item put in their place. The high-backed chair of the garrotte. Carefully made, Jan noticed in a cold and distant way, not done in a day. All well prepared. He had stopped, unconsciously, at the sight of it, his guard of Proctors stopping too.

This was a moment suspended in time, as though no one was sure just what to do next. The five judges, mute witnesses to their decision, stood on the platform. The crowd watched. Men, women, children, every inhabitant of the planet well enough to walk must have stood there, jammed in the Central Way. Silent as death itself, waiting for death. The perpetually overcast sky pressed down like a mourning blanket against the silence.

Broken suddenly by Chun Taekeng, never patient, always angry, immune to the emotions that gripped the others.

'Bring him over, don't just stand there. Let us get on with this.'

The momentary spell ended. The Proctors pushed Jan forward suddenly so that he stumbled against the lowest step and almost fell. It angered him; he did not want to be thought a coward at this moment. He pushed back hard against them, shrugging their hands from his arms. Free for the instant, he started up the steps by himself so that they had to hurry after him. The crowd saw this and responded with a gentle murmur, almost a sigh.

'Come forward. Sit there,' Chun Taekeng ordered.

'Don't I get to speak any last words?'

'What? Of course not! It is not ordered that way. Sit!'

Jan strode towards the chair of the garrotte, arms firmly gripped again by the Proctors. He saw only Chun Taekeng, The Hradil, the other judges, and an immense loathing welled up within him, forcing out the words.

'How I hate you all, with your stupid little criminal minds. How you destroy people's lives, waste them, subjugate them. You should be dying not me . . .'

'Kill him!' The Hradil ordered, raw hatred in her face for the first time. 'Kill him now, I want to see him die.'

The Proctors pulled at Jan, forcing him towards the garrotte, while he pulled back, trying to get to the judges, to somehow break free and wreak vengeance upon them. Every eye was upon this silent struggle.

No one noticed the man in the dark uniform who pushed through the crowd. They made way for him, closed ranks behind him, staring at the platform. He struggled through the jammed front ranks and climbed the steps, until he was standing on the platform itself.

'Release that man,' he said. 'This affair is now concluded.'

He walked slowly across the platform and took the microphone from Chun Taekeng's limp fingers and repeated the words so that everyone could hear them.

No one moved. There was absolute silence.

The man was a stranger. They had never seen him before.

The fact was an impossibility. On a planet where no one arrived, where no one left, every person was known by sight if not by name. There could be no strangers. Yet this man was a stranger.

Whether he meant to fire or not, Proctor Captain Scheer

started to raise his gun. The newcomer saw the motion and turned towards him, a small and sinister weapon ready in his hand.

'If you don't drop that gun I will kill you instantly,' he said. There was cold resolve in his voice and Scheer's fingers opened and the gun dropped. 'You others as well. Put your weapons down.' They did as ordered. Only when the guns were safely out of their reach did he raise the microphone and speak into it again.

'You other Proctors out there. I want you to know that there are men on all sides aiming weapons at you. If you attempt to resist you will be killed at once. Turn and see.'

They did, everyone in the crowd as well as the Proctors. Noticing for the first time the armed men who silently appeared on the tops of the buildings along the Central Way. They held long and deadly weapons equipped with telescopic sights, aimed downwards. There was no doubt that they would use them efficiently and quickly.

'Proctors, bring your weapons up here,' the echoing voice ordered.

Jan stepped forward and looked at the man, at the two other armed strangers who joined him on the platform, and felt an immense relief surge through him. Just for an instant. His execution might only have been postponed.

'You're from the ships,' he said.

The stranger put the microphone down and turned towards him. A grey-haired man with dark skin and burning blue eyes.

'Yes, we're from the ships. My name is Debhu. Release Kulozik at once,' he snapped at the Proctors who hurried to obey. 'We landed out on the Road about twenty hours ago. I'm sorry we had to wait until now to show up but we wanted everyone in one place at the same time. You would have been killed if they knew we were coming. There could have been fighting, more deaths. I'm sorry you had to go through this, with the death sentence hanging over you.'

'You're with the ships – but you're not Earth Commonwealth men!'

The words were torn from Jan in an explosion of hope. Something tremendous, incredible had happened. Debhu nodded slow agreement.

'You are correct. There have been . . . changes . . .'

'What are you doing here? Clear this platform!' Chun Taekeng's anger cut through the paralysis that had gripped them all. 'Give me that microphone and leave! This is not to be tolerated – '

'Guards. Move the judges back. Watch them closely.'

Burly men with ready guns moved swiftly at Debhu's order, pushing the shocked Elders into a group, facing them with weapons ready. Debhu nodded approval and spoke through the microphone again.

'People of Halvmörk, I would like your attention. The ships are late because of a change in a number of planetary governments. We will tell you more about this later. For now it is enough to know that the absolute power of the Earth authorities known as the Earth Commonwealth has been broken. You are free people. What that means will be explained to you. For now it is enough to know that a war is still being fought and there has been much starvation. Every grain of corn you have grown is needed and we are grateful for it. Now go to your homes and wait to be informed. Thank you.'

Their voices rose in a loud babble as they turned, walking away, calling out to each other. Some men tried to stay, technicians, friends of Jan's but were moved on their way by the men with guns, more and more of them appearing down the Central Way. Jan waited in silence; he had to know more before he spoke.

'You knew about my trial and the verdict?' Jan said. Debhu nodded. 'How?'

'There is an agent on this planet.'

'I know. Ritterspach. But he's dead now.'

'Ritterspach was only a tool. He just took orders. No, the real agent is well trained and has been working here for years. Reporting on the Security network scramble frequency. We seized some of their equipment and heard the messages when we came out of jumpspace. That's why we didn't announce our arrival.'

Jan was still stunned by the rush of events and found it difficult to assimilate all the new information so quickly. 'An active agent here? But who . . .?' Even as he phrased the question the answer was obvious. He turned about and stabbed his finger at the judges. 'There's your undercover agent, right there!'

'Yes, that's the one,' Debhu agreed.

The Hradil screamed shrilly and lurched forward at him, her hands raised, her nails like animal's claws ready to scratch and rend. Jan waited for her, stepping forwards to receive her, seizing her wrists and prisoning them, staring into her hate-torn face just inches from his own.

'Of course. My enemy. The shrewdest and most vicious person on this planet. Too intelligent to be from the low stock of the others. A creature of Earth. Willing to live a life in exile on this miserable planet in exchange for the power, the absolute power to rule as she wished, destroy whom she wished. Who reported secretly to the ships when they arrived so her masters on Earth would know how well she was doing here. Who would see that anyone died who stood in her way . . .'

'No problems until you arrived,' she shrieked, spittle flying. 'They warned me you were a suspected Disrupter, I was to watch you closely. Get evidence.'

She swayed as he shook her, slowly and carefully in order not to hurt her ancient bones. His voice was low and triumphant.

'They lied to you, don't you realize that? They know all about me, convicted me and sent me here. It was a death sentence for me – or this prison world. You were just my keeper, sending reports to them. But no more. Do you hear that, agent? We've won and you have lost. Doesn't that make you feel good?'

Jan felt terrible. The touch of her revolted him. He released her, pushed her away to the guards who caught her before she could fall. Turned his back on her, sickened by the corpse-touch of her skin.

'Not quite won everywhere,' Debhu said. 'But at least we can win here. When we leave I'm taking this woman with me. And that Proctor, the one who murdered your friend. This kind of rule by violence has to end. We are going to have trials, public trials that will be broadcast on every occupied planet. Justice will be done – unlike the sideshow this creature arranged. We hope that the trials, with punishment where due for those found guilty, will bring peace. Get rid of the old hatreds. There are going to be a lot of pieces to pick up when this thing is over. But the end is in sight. We're winning on all fronts except one. The planets are ours, that was the easiest part. No one ever enjoyed being ruled from Earth. The space fleet was spread thin and could be attacked on a planet by planet basis. Our surprise was sudden. Deprived of their bases and support the Earth fleet could only withdraw – but they were relatively unharmed in the battles. Hurt but not destroyed. Now they have returned to Earth, to guard the home world. Too tough a nut for us to crack.'

'Yet they in turn can't attack the planets – no spacer can hope to succeed in capturing a well defended planetary base.'

'Agreed – but we have the same problem as Earth. So right now we have a stalemate. Earth has reserves of food and minerals, but in the long run their economy, as it stands now, cannot exist without the planets.'

'Nor can we exist without them as well.'

'Quite true. Their material reserves are high – but not their food supplies. I doubt if they can produce enough food for their population, even with synthetics. The future is still in doubt. We've won the first battles but not the war. And our need for food is even more desperate than Earth's. We have no reserves. That was Earth policy. Starvation is very close – which is why we need the corn. At once. The cargo ships are in landing orbit now, they started down as soon as I sent the signal that the position was secure. We thank you for getting the corn here despite all of the problems. We'll start loading at once.'

'No,' Jan said grimly. 'That's not the way it is going to be at all. The corn will not be loaded until I say so.'

Debhu stepped back, startled, his gun swinging up by reflex.

'Kill me if you like. Kill us all. But the corn is ours.'

Chapter Twenty

Debhu's eyes were angry slits in his dark face. 'What are you getting at, Kulozik? We're fighting a war and we need that food – we must *have* that food. No one is going to stand in our way. I can take your life as easily as I saved it.'

'Don't threaten me – or brag about your war. We have been fighting a war too, against this alien world. And we brought this corn for you. It didn't get here by accident. If we had left it behind it would be ashes by now. These people are poor enough, but they lost what little they had for your sake. Their clothing, furniture, personal possessions, all left behind to make room for the corn you want to grab as though you had a right to it. It is *ours* – do you understand that? Good men died when we went back on the second trip, and I don't want to find out that they died in vain. You'll get the corn all right, but we have certain conditions attached to it. You are going to listen to our terms or you are going to have to shoot us. You'll get the corn all right, but it will be the last. The decision is up to you.'

Debhu stared at Jan closely, at the tight muscles and half-closed fists. For a long moment they stood that way, facing each other in silence. Until the anger faded from Debhu's face to be replaced by a half-smile. He grunted and the gun slipped from sight.

'You're a hard man, Kulozik, I can see that,' he said. 'I'll just have to talk to you. You have a point. It's been a busy morning. I guess you have as much of a right to the fruits of the rebellion as anyone. Not that we have very much. Let's go find your wife, who will probably want to see you, and have something to drink and talk it over.'

'Agreed!'

Alzbeta was beyond words, still not believing what had happened. She buried her face in his shoulder, holding him to her, crying and not realizing why.

'It's all right,' Jan said. 'All over. Things are not going to be the way they used to be – they are going to be far better. Now make some tea for our guest and I'll tell you why.'

He dug out a bottle of his alcohol distillate and poured some into the cups, hoping the tea would ameliorate the taste. Debhu's eyes widened when he sipped some.

'It takes getting used to,' Jan said. 'Shall we drink then? To sanity and a peaceful future.'

'Yes, I'll drink to that. But I would also like to know what your rebellion means.'

'No rebellion,' Jan said, draining his cup and setting it down. 'Just give and take. Equality. The people here are now no longer economic slaves and that will have to end. They will have to work for their freedom – and they have started already. They'll keep supplying all the food you need. But they want something in return.'

'We haven't much to give. There has been a lot of destruction, more than I wanted to admit in public. Chaos. We'll be centuries rebuilding.'

'All we need is simple equality and what goes with it. The Elders' rule will have to be ended. Not at once, it is the only system they know and nothing would work without it. But it will break down of its own accord. We want full contact with the rest of the Commonwealth – the rest of the planets. I want these people to see democracy at work and compare it to economic slavery. I want the children educated offworld. Not all of them, just the best. They'll bring back intelligence and ideas, then everything will have to change for the better. The Elders will not be able to resist forever.'

'You're asking a lot . . .'

'I'm asking very little. But it must begin at once. Just a few children to begin with, this trip. We'll probably have to tear them away from their parents. But they'll learn, like it or not, and will eventually understand why this had to be done. It will be hard for them, for all of us, because I am sure that education and information is as restricted on the outer planets as it is on Earth. But the facts are there. They will just have to be uncovered and understood. All of us must have free access to the heritage of Earth from which we have been deprived. On this world it will eventually mean the end of the stultifying culture that has been forced upon these people. The food we have been supplying has economic power, so we should have some return for our labours. The future must be different. The people here have played their lives out like puppets. Real enough to them perhaps, but just things on strings to the puppet-masters on Earth. The Hradil was the tool they used to make sure that there was no deviation from the empty roles everyone had been selected to play. We were nothing to them, less than machines, unimportant and replaceable parts of a great organic machine built to supply cheap and tasteless food for poor men's dinners. But no more. We'll supply the food, but we want human status in return.'

Debhu sipped at his fortified tea, then nodded.

'Well why not. You're not asking for much in the material way now, and that is what counts. Since we have very little to offer. But we'll take the children, find schools for them . . .'

'No. I'll take care of that. I'm going with you.'

'You can't!' Alzbeta shouted, a cry of pain. He took her hands.

'It will only be for a little while. I'll return, I promise you.

186

But out there now, in the turmoil, no one really cares about us. I'll have to fight for everything we receive. I know what this planet needs and I'll get it. Though I'm sure not one person out of a hundred here will appreciate it. I'll take their children away for education, introduce change, supply treasonous thoughts and they are not going to love me for it.'

'You'll go away and never come back,' she said, so quietly he could barely hear her.

'Don't believe that for a second,' Jan said. 'My life is here with you. On this strange twilight-and-fire world. Earth is part of my past. I love you and I have my friends here and – with some changes life could be most enjoyable. I'm only going now because there is no one else for the job. I'll try to be back before our son is born. But I can't promise that. But I *will* be back before the trains leave again, because I'll be bringing the supplies and replacements that will make that possible.' He looked over at Debhu. 'I don't imagine you brought pile rods or anything else we have to have?'

'Not really. There was chaos, you know. And the need for food was desperate. Most of the things on the manifests for this planet are of Earth manufacture.'

'See what I mean, Alzbeta? We are going to have to take care of ourselves now and I am going to have to start it all by myself. But it will work. People will always have to eat.'

There was a rising rumble of braking jets from above. The ships had arrived. Alzbeta stood and put the teapot on the tray.

'I'll make some more tea. I'm sorry if I doubted you, acted foolishly. I know that you will come back. You always wanted things to change here, everything. And maybe they will. No, I'm sure they will. But after the changes – will we be happy?'

'Very,' he said, and her smile answered his.

The teacups rattled in their saucers as the roaring rose and rose until conversation was impossible.

The ships had come at last.

THE WORLD'S GREATEST SCIENCE FICTION AUTHORS
NOW AVAILABLE IN GRANADA PAPERBACKS

Frederik Pohl

The Man Who Ate the World	85p	☐
Survival Kit	85p	☐
Drunkard's Walk	75p	☐
Man Plus	95p	☐
Gold At Starbow's End	40p	☐
The Age of the Pussyfoot	95p	☐

Thomas M Disch

The Genocides	85p	☐
Echo Round His Bones	75p	☐
Under Compulsion	95p	☐
Camp Concentration	95p	☐
The Puppies of Terra	75p	☐

Jack Vance

Trullion: Alastor 2262	85p	☐
Fantasms and Magics	75p	☐
The Blue World	60p	☐
The Pnume	50p	☐
Servants of the Wankh	40p	☐
City of the Chasch	40p	☐
The Houses of Iszm	65p	☐
The Languages of Pao	65p	☐
Son of the Tree	65p	☐
Star King	35p	☐

THE WORLD'S GREATEST SCIENCE FICTION AUTHORS NOW AVAILABLE IN GRANADA PAPERBACKS

Ursula K LeGuin

Orsinian Tales	75p ☐
The Wind's Twelve Quarters (*Volume 1*)	85p ☐
The Wind's Twelve Quarters (*Volume 2*)	95p ☐
The Dispossessed	95p ☐
The Left Hand of Darkness	95p ☐
The Lathe of Heaven	95p ☐
City of Illusions	95p ☐

Robert Silverberg

Earth's Other Shadow	75p ☐
The World Inside	75p ☐
Tower of Glass	60p ☐
Recalled to Life	50p ☐
A Time of Changes	50p ☐
Invaders from Earth	80p ☐
Master of Life and Death	75p ☐

J G Ballard

The Crystal World	75p ☐
The Drought	80p ☐
The Disaster Area	95p ☐
Vermilion Sands	60p ☐
Crash	95p ☐
High-Rise	60p ☐

THE WORLD'S GREATEST SCIENCE FICTION AUTHORS NOW AVAILABLE IN GRANADA PAPERBACKS

Ray Bradbury

Fahrenheit 451	95p	☐
The Small Assassin	50p	☐
The October Country	50p	☐
The Illustrated Man	95p	☐
The Martian Chronicles	95p	☐
Dandelion Wine	95p	☐
The Golden Apples of the Sun	£1.25	☐
Something Wicked This Way Comes	75p	☐
The Machineries of Joy	60p	☐
Long After Midnight	95p	☐
The Best of Ray Bradbury Gift Set	£3.40	☐

Keith Roberts

The Grain Kings	65p	☐
The Chalk Giants	75p	☐
Machines and Men	50p	☐
Pavane	40p	☐

All these books are available at your local bookshop or newsagent, or can be ordered direct from the publisher. Just tick the titles you want and fill in the form below.

Name ....

Address..

....

Write to Granada Cash Sales, PO Box 11, Falmouth, Cornwall TR10 9EN.

Please enclose remittance to the value of the cover price plus:

UK: 30p for the first book, 15p for the second book plus 12p per copy for each additional book ordered to a maximum charge of £1.29.

BFPO and EIRE: 30p for the first book, 15p for the second book plus 12p per copy for the next 7 books, thereafter 6p per book.

OVERSEAS: 50p for the first book and 15p for each additional book.

Granada Publishing reserve the right to show new retail prices on covers, which may differ from those previously advertised in the text or elsewhere.